THE GULLIVER MOB

Tall Tales from a Theatre Tour

ANTHONY MCDONALD

(thinly disguised as ANTHONY MOYLAN)

Anchor Mill Publishing

Anchor Mill Publishing

4/04 Anchor Mill

Paisley PA1 1JR

SCOTLAND

anchormillpublishing@gmail.com

Cover design by Anna Atkinson Copyright © 2016

For Sarah Parnaby

And remembering Tony

When Impresario Nathan McCaffrey unexpectedly needs to make a tax loss he sends a no-hope Musical version of Gulliver's Travels out on the road. The Gulliver Mob is an affectionately told, nostalgic tale of a C-list theatre tour as seen through the eyes of Ian, a rookie assistant stage manager. This show will never end up in London's West End or on Broadway. It will never visit the great touring venues of the UK but must set up, week by week, in small theatres in small towns of which McCaffrey has never heard … and that have never heard of McCaffrey. As the tour progresses events move from the absurd to the crazy … then to the surreal and beyond.

Author's Note

The action of this story takes place some twenty-five years ago. Few people used mobile phones or had access to email. The French still counted in francs.

Contrary to any expectations aroused by the cover there are no explicit sex scenes in this book.

On the other hand, no animals were injured in the writing of it.

While any resemblance between any of the cast of characters and real-life human beings, whether living or dead, is entirely coincidental. More's the pity.

Reviews by Amazon Kindle customers

Read with caution - May cause outbursts of unconstrained laughter. This is the funniest book I have read in a long time. I can't begin to describe how funny it is. It is truly a laugh out loud comedy. The stories are so absurd they require you to suspend your disbelief but the characters (or most of them) are so affectionately drawn you actually care about them. Works faster and is cheaper than an antidepressant. This author deserves to be well known. (MrsGWyllt - UK)

Not only did I really enjoy it, but I chuckled out loud to myself on many occasions and admired the skill of imagination and prose that created this ridiculous sequence of events. Quite honestly, it's a triumph. And so very clever. And different. I enjoyed this book immensely and urge anyone with the resemblance of a sense of you know what to have a go and read it (Charles C -UK)

It is a very funny book, and there are several laugh-out-loud moments in it; particularly the boardroom scene which had me in stitches. It put me in mind of an Ealing comedy or the early Norman Hudis scripted Carry Ons and I could see Margaret Rutherford or Alistair Simm playing roles. Just my cup of tea, thoroughly recommended. (Taran Geary - UK)

If This Is Monday...

Nathan McCaffrey, impresario, Lothario, raconteur and bon viveur, opened the door of the Lion room and crossed to the mantelpiece. Once there he rummaged in the bowl of pot-pourri for the packet of Lambert and Butler cigarettes that his secretary unsuccessfully tried to hide from him. He took out the one remaining cigarette and lit it. Then he replaced the empty packet among the fading, scented petals and left the room. As he closed the door behind him the ormolu clock in front of the gilt-framed mirror struck thirteen. It was nearly nine o'clock this Monday morning.

The Lion room would now stand silent until nine o'clock, when the clock would chime the first quarter past thirteen, and empty until Nathan required it for its principal purpose: to impress the people that Nathan wanted or needed to impress. Apart from the clock and the candlesticks the room boasted a large sash window that was hung with dusty red plush curtains that had been salvaged from a derelict theatre in the Scilly Isles and reduced to more manageable proportions by Mrs

McCaffrey and her sewing machine. The window gave onto one of Soho's less magnificent squares – which nevertheless afforded a home to two old plane trees, whose bark peeled endlessly: Nathan imagined them as two elderly but still competitive striptease artists.

Fading photographs of fading stars lined the Lion room's walls: portraits of men and women whose names lie forever beyond the reach of the tip of one's tongue. All were signed indecipherably and bore similar legends. Most were along the line of *To Nathan with Love* or *With Thanks* or *Remembering the First night to end all First Nights.* But there were a few ladies' portraits with inscriptions so direct that they had to be removed from the walls when Mrs McCaffrey was visiting.

There was flock wallpaper of four nearly matching designs: leftovers from Arsenic and Old Lace at Theydon Bois, Charlie's Aunt at Peterlee, Hay Fever at Didcot and The Importance of Being Earnest at Shipton-Under-Wychwood. There was even a wall-to-wall carpet cunningly assembled from relics of Not Now Darling at Newton-Aycliffe. So much for the Lion room, where the clock was once again gathering its strength to chime the unexpected.

By now Nathan McCaffrey was next-door in the Lamb room. It contained two desks that had never known a coat of polish, a single telephone, two battered filing cabinets, a shelf full of the classics of the theatre repertoire and, on the floor, an immense stack of wilted scripts that lay in that long Limbo between proud submission and ignominious rejection. They rested on a carpet that twenty years earlier had already been threadbare; it was only the weighty presence of these fag-ends of so many aspirations that saved the carpet from total disintegration. In one corner of this room was an alcove behind a bead curtain, where a sink lurked and a gas-ring was preserved like a prehistoric insect in an amber of spillages.

Here in the Lamb room Nathan grovelled before the people to whom he owed money, before the tax inspectors, before people to whom he had made promises that he had never fulfilled and never could. It overlooked the same sad square with its peeling plane trees, through a grimy window dressed only in some kitchen curtain cast-offs, courtesy once again of Mrs McCaffrey.

These premises had given Nathan sanctuary for more than twenty years. Situated at the shadier end of Wardour Street and on the less fashionable side they were nevertheless sandwiched most conveniently between the offices of Messrs Riskett, Spender, and Hope – the chartered accountants who audited Nathan's annual trading figures – and those of Murphy and Kelleher the boxing promoters ... for whose good offices Nathan had once or twice had occasion to be grateful when words had failed him in the cut and thrust of business altercation.

Now Nathan began to deal with the day's correspondence, writing in longhand all over his secretary's shorthand pads. The post had not yet arrived but it was Nathan's policy always to answer it before it did. He knew what was heading his way so, in anticipation, drafted the following letters.

To Moses Bros, Wigmakers.

Dear Sirs

The account to which you refer was settled by a cheque (no: 902307) posted from this office on 27th of last month. Its subsequent disappearance is no concern of mine. May I make it clear that I consider this matter closed and I do not intend to enter into any further correspondence over it.

Yrs. Etc.

To the manager, The Shires Theatre.

Dear Mr Williams

I note your objection to the posters. Should you wish to replace them at your own expense with something more to your taste I shall be most happy to withdraw them.

Yrs. Etc.

To Beaver Associates.

Dear Luke

Whatever your client's recollection of my conversation with him may be, either he is willing to understudy for the inclusive amount or he isn't. If the former, may I expect his signed contract by return? If the latter, I shall re-cast early next week. Do you have anyone else on your books who plays the balalaika?

Yrs. Etc.

Nathan's secretary of long standing, Bunjy, entered the room and hung up her coat. Then she slanted her way through the bead curtain to make tea for them both. While the kettle worked its way to the boil she opened the tea caddy and fished around for the packet of Sobranie cigarettes that Nathan kept hidden from her among the tea-leaves. She removed the last cigarette and lit it, abstractedly re-interring the empty packet among the leaves.

Emerging from behind the bead curtain a few minutes later she handed Nathan his coffee and took him through his diary for the day.

'Eleven o'clock. Meeting with Dahlia Woodlark to discuss rewrites.'

Nathan nodded.

'Production meeting for Yes We Have No Pyjamas, two thirty.'

Nathan nodded more vigorously.

Bunjy drew an audible breath. 'Box office returns and production accounts for Gulliver's Travels are waiting to be looked at.'

Nathan groaned.

'It's getting urgent,' Bunjy persisted. 'Mr Hope has telephoned twice. And Mr Riskett stopped me on the stairs.'

'Can't we just lose Gulliver somehow?'

'Don't look at me,' said Bunjy. 'It was your idea to send out a tour to lose money on.'

'Yes, all right,' said Nathan. 'It would be fine if we just lost money on it and everything went smoothly. But it presents me with problems at every turn. Where are they this week?'

Bunjy consulted the wall-planner that was illegible to all save her. 'They finished in Corbridge on Saturday. Today they open in Tonbridge. I don't know why you don't pick venues that are close together instead of simply having similar names.'

Holly

From Corbridge, nestling under Hadrian's Wall, to Tonbridge in the hop gardens of Kent was not an especially straightforward journey by train. Nathan was obliged, as producer of the Gulliver tour, to pay the cost of rail travel for his company, although he was not obliged to pay for any but the cheapest available ticket. And thanks to Bunjy's tireless researches he had managed to come up with a discount fare available only to travellers from Corbridge to Tonbridge who elected to travel during the hours of darkness on the night of a full moon, and when the date of the preceding Wednesday had been a multiple of three, for seven pounds forty-three pence per head. As everyone had always said of him, with a mixture of irritation and envy, Nathan was a very lucky man.

The company felt rather less lucky as their journey rattled them through the cold night to Leeds, then Grimsby (to take on fish) then Birmingham, Worcester (where the fish got off), Chelmsford and Oxford, with changes in the small hours at Victoria, Brighton and Gatwick. The moon was setting and the February sun was rising when they tumbled off the train at Tonbridge and all the cafés were closed.

'What,' said Toby, 'do we do next?' He was nearly forty so he usually spoke first.

'We look for Mrs Bush, that's what,' said Michael

who, though a mere twenty-nine, was soundly practical.

Mrs Bush's address was easy to find, and Mrs Bush too, for it presumably was she in the first-floor flat whose bell-push had her name above it, whose windows stood open despite the rawness of the morning, whose ghetto-blaster was delivering Radio 2 to the entire street, who was singing along to it in a tremulous mezzo voice, and whose doorbell unfortunately didn't work.

'Throw stones at the window,' said Michael.

'They'll go inside,' objected Ian, the youngest of the three men gathered on the pavement. 'Since all the windows are open. It wouldn't be a good way to begin.'

'It hasn't been a good way to begin already,' argued Michael.

'Relax,' said Toby. 'She's coming to the window.'

Blue-grey hair and glasses appeared in one of the open frames above them. 'Is that you, Jason?' queried the tremulous voice.

'No,' said Ian, 'It's Ian.'

'And Toby,' said Toby.

'And me,' said Michael.

'And who are you all supposed to be?' asked Mrs Bush.

'Dear God,' said Michael, 'she's one of those.'

'We're from the theatre,' explained Ian patiently. He was a tall, gangling, bespectacled lad of twenty-one, with a nose like putty and a mop of lank blond hair. He was the most junior stage manager among the company and, amazingly, was liked by everyone. It was his first job since leaving drama school. This week it had been his turn to book accommodation for the three of them. There was no particular reason for him to share digs with Toby and Michael, who had been an item since time immemorial, but he found their company congenial so he often did. 'We're the Gulliver company. We spoke on the phone. Remember?'

'No.'

'On Thursday. It is Mrs Bush, isn't it?'

'Yes.'

'You're on the digs list.'

'I'm what?'

'On the theatre's list of actors' accommodation.'

'Oh, all right. If you say so. Does that mean you're coming to stay?'

'Well yes. Aren't we expected?'

'Of course. Only not just yet. To tell the truth I'd forgotten you were coming. You couldn't make it next week, I don't suppose?'

'I don't think we could, Mrs Bush,' said Toby.

'You can call me Holly,' said Mrs Bush. 'I'd better let you come up then. Where's Jason?'

The blue rinse and glasses disappeared from the window and a few moments later Holly had unbolted the front door. 'You're the first I've ever had,' she said, surveying them wonderingly like a hen confronting her first hatchlings. 'Come on up.' They slow-marched upstairs. 'Sit down. Where *is* Jason. Hell, it's nearly nine o'clock. You'd better have a gin.' And so the new week began.

That night Holly forgot she had PGs staying and went to bed locking them out. Toby climbed the drainpipe – not because he was the youngest but precisely because he wasn't – and knocked on her window, frightening her half to death.

On Tuesday it was Michael's turn to have the broken fried egg for breakfast; on Wednesday, Ian's. Holly could fiy a maximum of two eggs without breaking the yolks: three was beyond her. Also on Tuesday Jason turned up to do the shopping. He was the ring-leader of a pack of twelve-year-olds who gave up a lot of their free time to help old ladies who lived alone. Jason did do the shopping but he forgot to return the change. On Wednesday afternoon Jason brought all his friends round to watch TV and smoke all Holly's cigarettes. On Thursday Toby had the broken egg, Holly smoked as many of Ian's cigarettes as she could find (by now Ian had discovered the necessity of hiding them all around the flat), Jason shopped again and Holly mislaid a twenty-pound note. On Friday she only lost a tenner.

It was Saturday morning and Ian was sitting on the sofa looking into The Sun. 'Eggs, eggs, oh eggs!' came Holly's injured voice from the kitchen. Ian looked up for a second, his nose twitching optimistically. 'Don't do this to me, eggs!' came from the kitchen in an urgent wail.

Toby and Michael came into the living-room, Toby still arranging the hair near his temples with his fingers. Michael asked, 'What's the news?'

'Dunno yet,' said Ian. 'I'm still on Page Three.'

'Breakfast up,' yelled Holly suddenly and powered into the room with two plates of egg, bacon and mushroom that were almost too hot for her to hold.

'My turn for the broken egg,' said Ian good-naturedly, taking the plate that harboured the more damaged one of the two.

'That ain't the broken egg,' said Holly. 'You wait till you see the broken egg.' She went back into the kitchen to fetch it, reappearing as she routinely did with the third plate of breakfast in her left hand and a glass of vodka and tonic in her right. She put the plate on the table, leaving the men to decide which was whose, and retired to the sofa to watch them eating while she sipped her well-earned reward.

After breakfast they stayed put, smoking cigarettes, because as it was Saturday no-one had a call in the morning. Not even Ian.

'What does a call mean?' asked Holly.

'It means work,' said Ian with a smile. 'Your call is the time you start. Today my call is one o'clock. For Toby and Michael it's five minutes to two.'

'Why's yours earlier?' asked Holly, brows furrowing above her tumbler.

'Because I'm less important, so naturally I work longer hours for less money,' said Ian.

'That figures,' said Holly, nodding.

'I'm an ASM,' said Ian. 'That stands for Assistant Stage Manager.'

'Meaning…?'

'That I'm a dogsbody. But…' His eyes brightened. 'I'm also an understudy on this tour. Which means that I'd be very important indeed suddenly if anybody broke a leg or had flu. Unfortunately that hasn't happened yet. But at least it means I have one foot on the second rung of the ladder.'

Holly found she had another question. 'What about this play you're doing then? Oliver's Troubles?'

'Gulliver's Travels,' Michael corrected gently. 'The Rock Musical version.'

'I mean,' pursued Holly, 'is it any good? The local press said it was appalling. Now of course I'm not the sort of person who believes everything they read in the…'

'The papers were right,' said Michael. 'It is appalling. It's under-funded, mis-conceived, badly adapted and full of bad songs.'

'It's said to be the worst thing on the touring circuit for three and a half years,' said Ian with pride.

'But,' said Toby, 'we actors have a fatal optimism. We are always hoping…'

'Like Mr Micawber…' interjected Michael.

'For something…' added Ian.

'To turn up,' said Toby.

'A better part,' said Michael

'A better show,' said Ian.

'Good money,' said Michael.

'Fame,' said Toby.

'To be able to wear dark glasses and still be recognised in the street,' said Ian.

There was a ring at the doorbell and a moment later Jason was in the room.

'Jesus,' said Toby, 'he even has his own key!'

'Can anyone lend my mum a fiver?' Jason wanted to know. 'She's really stuck this week.'

Holly groped in her purse and before you could say gin five pounds and Jason were all gone.

'You know something, Holly,' said Michael conversationally, 'you're crazy. You let those kids rob you, cheat you, smoke your cigarettes – and our cigarettes. Another six months and they'll be at the vodka bottle. Don't you see? Every penny we're paying you for staying here is going into their bottomless little pockets.'

'They're good kids,' said Holly, dropping her glass in her agitation. 'Just a bit careless, that's all.'

'You know that's not true,' said Toby gently.

Holly sank back on the sofa, ignoring the dropped, spilt glass. 'What would you do if you were me? Living all alone since my husband left me. At first I thought I could live in the past but in time it got too big for me. All that past and only me rattling around in it. Wouldn't you want the company of visitors? And if you couldn't get good ones wouldn't you be grateful for bad ones – like you lot with your acting roles? I bet you would.' Holly dabbed with a handkerchief at the vodka that had spilled across the sofa, and then applied the hanky to her eyes. 'If it wasn't for those kids…'

'I have an idea,' said Ian.

Toby and Michael exchanged glances. It was the first

time in the month they'd known him that Ian had said anything like this.

Ian dashed back to Holly's house between the matinee and the evening show. A little breathlessly he explained what he'd arranged. The theatre management had agreed to notify Holly directly as soon as each theatre tour arrived in town, to save her the trouble of remembering for herself. They would offer visiting actors a cut-price rate on her behalf. In return, her theatrical paying guests would help with occasional shopping in the mornings. Holly would have company throughout the week, a regular income, and – with any luck – would not get robbed.

'But,' Ian cautioned, 'you must promise to give the boys the boot.'

Holly promised.

'I'll phone on Monday to check,' Ian said, as sternly as he knew how. (So not as sternly as all that.)

'You have to take your hat off to him,' said Michael to Toby later. 'To come up with an idea like that. To carry it out…'

'To sweet-talk the theatre management…'

'And on a Saturday afternoon…'

'I know,' said Toby, nodding sagely. 'That's the most amazing part.'

'But he'll need to be careful,' said Michael. 'Trying to do good around the place...'

'Indeed,' said Toby. 'It seldom has quite the results that you expect...'

Policy and the Art of Casting

'It makes no sense,' said Ian to Toby. 'No sense at all.' They were sitting on the floor of the half-built stage set at Slimbridge that next Monday morning drinking tea. 'The advance bookings are only eight percent. At Tonbridge they stood at eleven percent on the Monday morning and at Corbridge they were at ten. That can't cover the wages. It was the same in January. It's going to be the same here. Why does he keep it going? That's what I'd like to know.'

'What did you have for breakfast?' Toby asked him.

'This morning?' Ian rummaged among his short-term memories. 'Muesli, I think.'

'Did you have to borrow money to pay for it?'

'No,' said Ian. 'I've actually paid off my overdraft since the tour started.'

'Then that's all right,' said Toby, beginning to smile. 'Wages coming in every week... That's all you actually need to know. No point wanting to know anything else.'

Philip the stage manager arrived suddenly on stage with them: a blaze of red hair, wild eyes and long teeth. He had news he was itching to impart. He looked at them both in turn then, sitting down on the floor next to them with a bump, said with gleeful relish, 'You know those new jazz shoes Nick ordered?' Nick was the company manager, Philip's immediate boss.

'Yes,' said Toby. 'Haven't they come?'

'Oh yes, they've come all right.'

'Six pairs?' queried Ian.

'Yup.'

'Correct sizes? Even a pair big enough for Susan?' Susan was the leading lady of the production and on the tall side.

Philip nodded.

'So what's the problem?' Toby asked.

'They've all got two left feet.' Philip threw himself back across the stage floor and rolled there, an untidy bundle of teeth, hair and duffle-coat, weeping with laughter at a situation that, for the moment at least, was somebody else's problem to sort out.

In the Lion room at Nathan McCaffrey's Wardour Street premises was to be found one item of furniture which has not featured in this story yet. Associated as much with the rooms of psychiatrists as with those of film and theatre producers, it was perhaps too obvious a piece of equipment to need special mention. But it was on the cushions of this piece of property that the following conversation took place that morning, before Susan, who had spent the weekend in London, had to travel away to rejoin the company for evening curtain-up at Slimbridge..

'I need you, Susan.'

'I know that, Nathan.'

'It wouldn't be the same without you, Susan.'

'It's really sweet of you to say that, Nathan, but…'

'Darling. I'd be lost without you. Honestly, I could never find another giantess like you.'

'That may be true,' agreed Susan, sprawling a little. 'But the role of Glumdalclitch is so very limiting. You say you're going to take my career in hand. Surely you agree that I need a bit of …stretching.'

Nathan peered past the face he was just then dusting with kisses, taking in the six-foot-three figure that was folded next to him on the couch. He didn't think that stretching was quite what Susan needed most… 'There'll be time for all that soon enough,' he said. 'Hedda Gabler…Mother Courage…'

'I wasn't thinking quite as far ahead as Mother Courage just yet,' said Susan. 'I was thinking more about Binky…'

'I know, Darling. But Binky isn't really any bigger than Glumdalclitch. As a role, I mean.' Nathan added that last part hastily. Susan, though admirably cast as the young giantess, could on occasion be touchy about her stature.

'It's not just the part, Nathan, it's the prestige. The pre-West-End tour, the First Night, Yes We Have No Pyjamas reviewed in the Nationals... Introducing Susan Shearwater as Binky. The Long West End run. Do you think it might last as long as The Mousetrap?'

'Yes it might. Of course it might.' Nathan licked the inside of Susan's left ear delicately. 'But would you really want to go on playing Binky for forty years?'

'If it kept us working together, Nathan, oh yes!'

Really, Nathan thought, this young generation of actresses was quite extraordinary. Extraordinarily wonderful. Such commitment to their art. He thought of his daughter, now at seventeen just four years younger than Susan and already yearning to begin her own acting career. Would she too demonstrate such commitment? And in such a fashion? He put the uncomfortable thought from his mind. As long as he remained in business as an impresario no daughter of his would ever need to go looking for work on anyone else's Lion room couch.

'We'll go on working together anyway,' Nathan murmured reassuringly in Susan's ear. 'Whether you play Binky or not. There'll be a lot of summer work coming up...'

'I know,' said Susan. 'I just keep hoping for... Well, you know... Something a bit more than just end-of-the-pier.'

'But all my shows are more than just end-of-the-pier.

However humble the venues in which they may find themselves they have qualities about them...' He tried to think what qualities. With some success. 'They have ineffability,' he went on. 'Numinosity...' He knew that Susan wouldn't dare ask what the long words meant. Otherwise he wouldn't have used them. He had no idea himself.

'I realise that of course,' said Susan suavely. 'But one has to keep certain objectives in mind when planning a career. Does one not?'

'Of course. But there's going to be at least two new tours going out in the autumn. On of them is simply bound to Go In. There'll be lots of goodies for you, my angel...'

'For example?'

'Well, for example... Look, these things are rather under wraps at the moment and we can go into them another time. But, for example ... er ... there's going to be a play about a boy and girl who ... um ... meet but whose families aren't hitting it off and who die in a suicide pact...'

'You mean you're going to do Romeo? How wonderful! And I'd get to play...'

'Well no, not exactly. Touring Shakespeare does work out rather expensive. It's all those damned swords. No, it isn't Romeo. But it'll be a play on roughly the same lines. Very similar in fact.'

'It sounds great. Who's written it?'

'Someone, someone. I don't know yet. It'll be in that pile on the floor in the other room, the pile I haven't looked at yet. Probably among the top six. There may be more than one.'

'I see,' said Susan. She couldn't keep a tinge of disappointment out of her voice or the little roll she did with her shoulders.

'No, but really,' said Nathan. 'I never read a script without thinking of you.' That may have been true. Nathan hardly ever read a script.

'Do you? Honestly?'

'Honestly.' Nathan licked the inside of Susan's right ear.

'That tickles. All the same, it's still Binky that I really want.' She turned her body towards him. 'More than anything else in the whole world.' Susan began to undo the buttons of her blouse. 'I want to play Binky.'

'Then you shall, my Darling…'

'Oh Nathan!'

'You shall of course, my love.'

'Oh!'

'Provided only that Gulliver is finished before the casting of Yes We Have No Pyjamas is finalised.'

'Oh!!'

'Well. You know I couldn't possibly afford to lose my Glumdalclitch, don't you?'

'Yes, but...'

'Gulliver won't go on for ever, you know.'

'Sometimes I...'

'Now listen. I've promised as much as I can. I can't say fairer than that, can I?'

'I suppose...' But Susan's lips were prevented from further comment by the pressure against them of Nathan's own.

What Susan did not know and never would, what none of the Gulliver company knew, not even Runjy, who unlike the others was party to the secret that Gulliver was out on tour in order to make a loss for fiscal housekeeping reasons, was that Gulliver had to keep touring for a further reason. Gulliver had to keep travelling until Yes We Have No Pyjamas was safely cast and in rehearsal because the part of Binky had already been promised – on this very couch – to a young maid called Marian, the newest, youngest and brightest star in Nathan's firmament. Marian, at the age of only nineteen, had learnt a lesson about the Lion room couch that twenty-one-year-old Susan had yet to take on board. That you should get the contract first. Only then should you lie on it.

A Pool Party

By the time the whole cast was assembled at Slimbridge that Monday afternoon there was a note to be found in everyone's pigeonhole. It said: *The Playgoers' Association and Supporters' Club invites each and every member of the Gulliver's Travels company to an after-show pool party at Courtenay House, Shuttle Hangar Lane. Refreshments provided. Bring costume. Lucinda Reeve, Secretary.*

'We can save on fish and chips tonight, then,' said Philip, rubbing his hands in anticipation. 'And we're not even asked to bring a bottle. Could be good.'

'But what about this costume thing?' said Susan. 'I have eight. Which one should I take?'

'Take them all,' said Toby. 'I'm taking all mine.'

'That's easy for you,' said Susan with a sniff. 'You only have seven. And since you often complain that you have to carry the show, carrying seven costumes shouldn't come as a great hardship.'

'I think Susan's spent the weekend in the knife drawer,' said Fran. Fran only had three roles herself. But she was also kept pretty busy as an assistant stage manager. 'But seriously, what do they want us to do? Bring costumes is all very well but…'

'I know,' said Susan decisively. 'We'll get a ruling

from Nathan. He'll know what we should do.' And she went off to phone him.

'What do they mean by a pool party anyway?' Fran asked.

'Obviously it's a big house with a billiard room,' said Michael, shrugging his shoulders in a knowledgeable sort of way.

'Billiards in costume?' Fran queried. 'It sounds bizarre.'

'Wait and see,' said Toby. 'And in good time all shall be revealed.'

'I shouldn't pin too much hope on its being that sort of party either,' said Fran.

'Nathan says,' said Susan, returning from the pay-phone by the stage door, 'to wear whichever costume we like, so long as we don't go asking for them to be specially cleaned or ironed in the morning. He also said we weren't all to go as Struldbruggs in case people had heart attacks or cancelled their bookings.'

'I wasn't thinking of going as a Struldbrugg,' said Michael. 'You might as well go to a party dressed as the Elephant Man.'

'How are we supposed to be getting there anyway?' asked Toby. 'Has anybody thought about that?'

'I suppose,' said Ian, 'that people who have cars…'

'…Will be expected to take the people who haven't as usual,' finished Susan and her opposite number Peter together. They were the only two people in the company who had their own transport. 'And getting home again? I'm not playing taxi-driver…' they said this in unison too '…to a crowd of drunks in fancy-dress after midnight in a place I've never driven in before.'

'Oh stop that,' said Michael. 'What does it matter how we all get home? We can think about that when we get there.'

Surprisingly Michael's refusal to worry about the transport issue proved justified. After that evening's performance they were met by taxis at the stage door, with the additional promise that taxis would be forthcoming to take them home again later at no cost to themselves. Susan wore her Glumdalclitch costume – the one with the vertical stripes that emphasised her height. Toby went as a Struldbrugg because, as he said, somebody ought to. Michael went in his costume as Lilliputian Minister for the Environment, and he took his tightrope as well in case he should be asked to walk across it. He had discovered early in life the need to be attentive to these details. He had learned the harp as a boy and once been greatly surprised at being asked to play it at a children's party. His hosts had seemed no less surprised when he told them he hadn't brought it with him. Since then he had always gone to parties well prepared … if not always for the right thing.

Courtenay House, Shuttle Hangar Lane, was a handsome building in Stockbroker's Tudor style. Presumably it had a large garden though, since they arrived in the dark, it was hard to guess how far it extended. They approached the front entrance across a gravel sweep and when the door was opened they were shown into a vast living-room where a polite knot of people of middle age, size and class was gathered at one end while a table, laid with an impressive array of hot and cold dishes, stood at the other. The new arrivals, well practised in the ways of supporters' club suppers, contrived to smile vaguely into the knot of people while inching their way imperceptibly but inexorable towards the table. Which the stage management and technical crew – for once at an advantage over their actor colleagues in being unencumbered with bulky costumes – reached first. Intent as they were on their objective they could not help noticing a look of something like surprise on the collective face of the polite knot opposite.

'Hello,' said someone detaching herself from the group and advancing with outstretched hand towards Susan – for the excellent reason that Susan was the tallest person present and was wearing the closest thing to normal dress. 'Call me Lucinda. I once knew Dame Edith Evans.'

'What a pleasure that must have been for Dame Edith,' said Susan smoothly. 'I'm the Leading Lady. Call me Susan.'

Dogs began barking somewhere outside and then

came something that sounded like a human yell, followed by more barking. Nobody remarked on this or took any notice.

'How interesting that you've all come in your theatrical attire,' said Lucinda. 'We are all most pleasantly surprised.'

'Well, you shouldn't be too surprised,' said Susan sweetly. 'It did say bring costumes on the invitation.'

'Did it now?' Lucinda's surprise at this seemed genuine.

'It also said it was going to be a pool party. As you can see, some of the boys have brought their own billiard cues and balls.' She pointed across the room to where Ian and Peter stood, holding their cues like a pair of riflemen. They weren't their own cues exactly. They'd been borrowed from the stage door pub for the evening …without the fuss and complication of asking. Susan fished her now crumpled invitation out from among the folds of her striped costume and showed it to Lucinda.

Lucinda looked at it. 'Oh dear. How silly of us. We must have had some cards left over from last summer. You see, in the summer we do invite the actaws to have a swim with us. Costume, you see, means swimming costume and pool, of course… Well, anyway. I hope you won't be too disappointed. You see, the pool's an outdoor one.'

'I don't think anyone'll be too upset,' said Susan. 'As

you can see, we're none of us really dressed for bathing.'

'We could have a walk to the pool perhaps, after everyone's eaten. Even walk across it if the ice is firm enough.'

'That would be lovely,' said Susan. 'Such an imaginative end to the evening.'

Then someone else came up to talk to Susan. This was a very tall lady who asked a little breathlessly if being so tall wasn't a handicap in the theatre. Susan replied demurely that she thought it wasn't, since we were all the same height lying down, weren't we?

A man was talking to Fran. He managed to forget her name three times during the first two minutes of their conversation. He wondered how actors managed to remember all their lines. Fran said that in her case there was no difficulty as she only had twenty-seven and a half to remember and had been saying them every night except Sundays for the last three months. 'But that's even more impressive,' the man said. 'Three months without forgetting a single one!'

'It's like remembering your phone number, or to clean your teeth,' said Fran.

The man raised his eyebrows expressively and sighed. 'I wish,' he said. 'My phone's been disconnected for ages. I never could remember to pay the bills. As for my teeth … they haven't been my own since I don't remember when. But to come back to… Oh now, where were we?' He laughed. 'You see, you have such distracting blue eyes if you don't mind my saying so…'

Linda the wardrobe mistress found herself enmeshed in conversation with an elderly woman who asked her if theatre costumes weren't exorbitantly expensive these days. Linda had already ascertained, with a quick and practised eye, that the woman had made her own party frock out of a set of old cushion covers, cutting away the worn bits.

'Well, yes,' they are,' said Linda. 'But we can do no end of things with old cushion covers. And then there's so much more nudity these days. Such a godsend to a low-budget outfit like ours.'

'Nudity in Gulliver's Travels?' The woman sounded astonished.

'No, actually there isn't. But we're benefitting indirectly from Mr McCaffrey's new venture which will open in London, all being well, in April. Yes, We Have No Pyjamas. You could say we were getting their cast-offs. Financially speaking, I mean…'

An earnest lady asked Ian if he didn't think Gulliver's Travels an unusual choice for a rock musical. He asked her if she hadn't asked the same question about St John's Gospel when Jesus Christ Superstar had come out many years previously. She nodded, impressed by his seriousness. 'And now I come to think of it, they made The Ten Commandments into a film, didn't they?' She shook her head. 'Though I can't help feeling the original tablets were better.'

Then ... but suddenly the food was seen to have run out and everyone began to make going-home noises. Lucinda announced that she would lead a quick tour around the swimming pool in the garden while the taxis were on their way. Everyone trooped outside. Ian asked around as to the whereabouts of Toby and Michael. Nobody had seen them. Some people guessed they had decided not to come after all.

The swimming pool, which was lit by a ring of fairy-lights, had a tarpaulin cover over it. Lucinda insisted shrilly that it should be removed, despite her guests' unanimous insistence that this was quite unnecessary.

'A pool party is what you were promised, and a pool party is what you shall have,' she said in a fairy-godmotherly sort of way, waving her arms about in the same sort of fashion. Two men were instructed to peel back the tarpaulin, which they gravely did. This action revealed an opaque sheet of ice which would have been featureless in the extreme but for the presence of one large object in the centre which stuck up through the ice like a pie-funnel through pastry. It was the glassy head of a dead cow, complete with horns and staring eyes.

'That will do,' Lucinda said grandly. 'You can cover it up again now.' The two men rolled the tarpaulin back over the top of everything without a flicker of anything on their faces. 'Remind me to talk to Jorrocks,' she said to one of them. 'He gets more careless each year. I do wish he'd use the skimmer more thoroughly. Last year he overlooked two wood pigeons – the year before, a pheasant and a badger.'

A few snowflakes fell among the fairy-lights and then the merciful sound of taxis hooting could be heard from the gravel sweep at the front.

'Lucinda's a treasure,' said Fran to Susan. 'That cool, that sang-froid. She must have been a professional.'

'She told me she once knew Dame Edith,' said Susan.

'Ah,' said Fran. 'That would account for it.'

It was at the moment when everyone was settled in their taxis and their respective drivers asked them, 'Where to?' that the unpleasant truth dawned that everyone's day clothes, house keys, wallets and purses were locked in the dressing-rooms at the theatre, and would have to remain there, in theory at least, until five thirty the following afternoon.

Double Entry

After a certain amount of negotiation the taxi drivers agreed to take the actors to the theatre in three of the cabs and to take the stage management, who were quite normally dressed, to the police station in the fourth one – to report the problem. The actors were to await developments.

But after ten minutes of playing I-spy outside the theatre in the lightly falling snow there had been no developments and the taxi drivers had withdrawn. They were disinclined to wait indefinitely on people who not only had no money in their pockets but no pockets either.

Peter grew tired of playing I-spy in conditions of such poor visibility. He left the others and walked round the building, returning a few minutes later, quite excited because he had found a small window, not too high up, that wasn't properly fastened. He thought it would be a good idea to make an entry through it and then unlock the stage door from the inside. And since Peter not only played the role of Gulliver himself, as well as being able to sing an impressive top B flat into the bargain everybody naturally agreed with him and they all went round the block to try.

Peter himself was much too big to climb through the small window, which opened – they guessed – into an office store cupboard. But Fran climbed up onto his shoulders and, with a little help from a handy drainpipe, got her head inside. This triggered an alarm though no-one knew this: there was no vulgar whistling or ringing of bells, only a light flashing on a screen at the police station.

'What can you see?' Peter called up Fran's legs.

'There's a filing cabinet or something. I should be able to jump down onto it without hurting myself. I think the room *is* a cupboard but there seems to be an open door leading into an office. Hold on a minute. Can you look after my skirt for me?' She unzipped it neatly and it fell around Peter's shoulders like a scarf. Then Fran reached up again for the window and squeezed her head and shoulders in, then one leg. 'Wow, that's difficult.' Her voice came muffled from inside. 'And I can't reach the filing cabinet for the moment. I'll just rest a minute. Get my breath back.'

It seemed a long minute. But at the end of it everyone's attention was distracted by the arrival of a car which stopped beside them. A man got out and shone a torch on Peter. The beam lingered especially on the skirt around his neck.

'Good evening, sir,' said a voice from behind the torch. 'Having a spot of trouble are we? Women's clothes are so difficult for a man to wear gracefully, I always think.'

'Oh, good evening, officer,' said Peter.

'Would that by any chance be a lady's leg protruding

from the wall above your head?'

'Well, as a matter of fact…'

'I think you'd better step around this corner,' said the policeman rather firmly, and he led the group, with the exception of Fran of course, a quarter of the way round the building then beamed his torch up the wall.

'Good God!' said Peter.

'I suppose,' said the policeman musingly, 'they can't both belong to the same woman?'

For there, sticking out at right angles from a small window about eight feet above the ground, was another leg.

'But whose is it?' asked Susan.

'If you don't know,' said the policeman, 'then I'm sure I don't.'

From around the next corner there suddenly appeared the entire stage management team plus Toby and Michael. Toby and Michael each had one hand swathed in bandages. Michael was also wearing a skirt around his neck.

'We've been going round in circles looking for you lot,' said Toby. 'There's another leg round the other side, by the way. Do you know anything about that?'

'It's Fran's,' said Peter. 'Whose is this one?'

'Natasha's.'

'Who the hell's Natasha?'

'She's the theatre publicity manager.'

'And that's her idea of publicity?'

'It's a long story…'

'I am now going to open the front door of the theatre,' said the policeman. 'I shall then shut my eyes and count to ten very slowly. When I open them you will have disappeared. Completely. All of you. Do you understand? Then I shall drive away. And I don't want to see any of you or your associated legs again. Ever.' The policeman turned the key in the lock and at that moment there was a flash from across the road. A neighbour had taken a photograph.

By the end of the next hour the following things had happened. the theatre had been entered and the two ladies rescued; the neighbour – a local photographer whose name was Butcher – had been persuaded to develop his photos in his own dark-room; Natasha had put her skirt back on and unlocked the theatre office drinks cabinet. Now she was busy at her secretary's typewriter tapping out a press release about the evening's adventures.

'I still don't understand what happened to Toby and Michael,' said Susan.

'It was our taxi driver,' Michael explained. 'He didn't take us to Courtenay House: he made a mistake, so we arrived at the house next door. So when we rang the bell...'

'...Dressed respectively as a creature time forgot and a politician with twenty metres of rope...' interjected Toby.

'...The people who came to the door, an elderly couple, were a bit...'

'But it all happened very quickly,' added Toby. 'They had two spaniels. One went for Michael, the other one...'

They both held out their bandaged wrists.

'There was a lot of noise,' said Toby. 'I'm surprised you didn't hear it.'

'We did,' said Susan sedately.

'We sorted it all out in the end,' said Michael. 'Everyone apologised to everyone else. Toby even offered to pay to have the spaniels cleaned.'

'Why?' asked Peter.

'He bled all over them. They'd been white originally. But apparently you can't dry-clean a spaniel.'

'So they drove us to the hospital to have stitches.'

'And the doctor who did the sewing was a personal

friend of Natasha's. So he phoned her and asked her to come and collect us…'

'Which she did, and on the way here we spotted the stage management coming out of the police station. So we picked them up and brought them here with us. Only it was very dark and Natasha had a job trying to get the key into the lock on the stage door.'

'So I tried…' said Philip cheerfully.

'Yes,' said Toby. 'And ended up dropping the whole bunch of keys into an open drain.'

'My hands were cold,' Philip explained.

'Anyway, that's why…'

'OK, thank you,' said Natasha, removing the press release from the typewriter with a flourish. 'We've got quite enough.'

'But what about a headline?' asked Ian. 'Anybody got any ideas?'

'What about Local Pig Saves Gulliver's Bacon?' suggested Philip.

'No thank you,' said Natasha. 'First of all, you can't make rude remarks about the police in a town like Slimbridge. People'd set fire to the theatre. Secondly, that cop was extremely nice to you. Thirdly, although local press love to have their articles ready-made for them in the form of press releases they don't like you to supply the headlines as well. They go all funny on you and end up not printing anything…' Natasha turned to the photographer. 'More Bristol Cream, Mr Butcher?'

The press release was delivered to the offices of the local newspaper at three o'clock in the morning. The story, complete with photo of the theatre with protruding legs, appeared in the afternoon edition. Theatre bookings went up by geometric progression and by the end of the week capacity had topped seventy-nine percent. The supporters' club had been along. The whole hospital staff had turned out. Even Lucinda Reeve's next-door neighbours had come out for an evening at the theatre, their unusual liver-spotted spaniels attracting much admiring attention from fanciers.

'It's a blip,' said Nathan, studying the figures. He turned his attention to the enclosed newspaper clipping. 'What the hell's this?' He looked at the pictures of the Slimbridge theatre with its attendant legs and read out the caption. It ran: *About those Hams in the Window, Mr Butcher*…

'They don't do headlines like they used to,' said Nathan.

A Regional Issue

'What have you done about digs for next week?' Fran asked Ian one day towards the end of the week in Slimbridge. They would be heading up to the windswept north-east coast of England – to a town whose name for once didn't end with the syllable bridge.

'Staying with Toby and Michael again. At twenty-seven Battle Cruiser Terrace. With a Mrs More.'

'Then we shall be neighbours,' said Fran. 'Susan and I are at number twenty-eight. With a Mrs Much.'

As it turned out the whole company stayed in Battle Cruiser Terrace, a line of six-storey mansions that had been built in a time when battle cruisers and other ships were big business in the north-east. Now the houses were sadly down-at-heel though they still possessed a dignity that the new poverty could not dispel. Laurels might overhang neglected paths in overgrown front gardens but a set of eight grand steps still led up to each massive front door.

Mrs Much and Mrs More were sisters, both widowed and both severely incapacitated by arthritis. They lived on weak tea with lots of milk and sugar in it. This paid for, but only just, by the profits from the theatrical lodgings business they ran together, using their large, slowly crumbling houses for the purpose. Each widow had withdrawn over the years into a smaller corner of her establishment, as an ageing snail might, so that each now occupied only a tiny corner of her basement, leaving a truly enormous number of rooms to let. They had a near monopoly of digs in the town because they charged minimal prices in return for maximum dilapidation and could not be undercut. Neither woman had managed to get up to her top floor for nearly five years and neither had been to the theatre since their two husbands had died from separate heart attacks during the same negotiation with the Oil Pressure Gauge Makers' Union towards the end of the nineteen seventies.

Not many other people had been to the town's huge theatre since those heady days and it did not appear from the advance bookings that Gulliver's arrival was going to change the habits of a generation. When Philip examined the figures on Monday morning he saw that only twenty-two seats had been sold for the entire week and that nineteen of those were at concessionary prices. Four more tickets had been given to the local press and that was it. The runaway success of Slimbridge seemed more like two years ago than the two days that it in fact was.

On Monday afternoon the stage management and technical crew fitted up. That is, they erected the scenery, adjusted the lighting rig, and wired up the sound system of the theatre to meet the requirements of the incoming production. In the middle of this fit-up, above the din of hammers, sound-level checks and occasional cursing, the wailing of sirens was heard in the street outside. Nobody inside took any notice. The stage is a charmed rectangle and nothing that takes place beyond its perimeter impinges directly on it – at any rate, not until someone has written a play about it.

Still, when the stage crew left the building at five o'clock for their fish and chip break they could not help noticing that the premises next door, a tailor's shop, had burnt to the ground. Well, not quite. The walls still stood and part of the roof but nothing else was left. The shop was empty, black and cavernous. The pavement outside was a puddle of water and carbon. Two fire engines still lingered by the kerbside and a detachment of firemen was retrieving, one by one, some charred and naked tailor's dummies and throwing them unceremoniously into the gutter. Some children, smartly groomed for an afternoon's shopping, tugged at their parents' sleeves as they passed.

'Ee look,' they said, 'that shop's been burnt. T' firemen are throwing t' dead people out.'

'Oh aye,' replied the parents without bothering to correct the misapprehension as they walked on.

Toby, Michael and Ian had three small rooms like cupboards on the sixth floor of number twenty-seven. Two other members of the company, Jim the Giant and Edward the Musical Director, had rooms underneath. Up on the sixth floor there was a mansard roof that seemed to slope, bulge and buckle in all directions at once. The three little rooms opened into a small shared sitting-room whose ceiling was stained with water everywhere except where the plaster had already fallen off to expose the laths behind it. Under the worst-hit area stood a television and under the television – not on but under – stood a large washing-up bowl full of water.

'Do you really think,' said Toby as he emptied the bowl into the sink, 'that the bowl was put there to catch the water after it had poured into the top of the television and out the bottom? And why leave the thing in that corner? Do you suppose it works?'

'I'm going to switch it on and see,' said Michael. 'Stand well back, everyone.'

To their surprise the machine worked tolerably well. A black and white picture appeared after about thirty seconds and a few wisps of steam emerged from the back about a minute after that but they soon died away while the picture stayed. Toby replaced the empty bowl, this time on the top of the set.

In the night it rained heavily. The water entered at several points in the ceiling and left puddles on the coffee table and the draining-board and a wet patch at the corner of Ian's bed. Unsurprisingly the bowl on the television set was empty but just as they made this discovery Jim the Giant arrived from downstairs.

'What have you been up to?' he asked a little crossly. 'Water's been trickling through my ceiling all night. Right over the chair I'd put my chest expanders on. It's made the springs go all rusty.' Jim did a few calculations with his feet and announced that the water had entered his room immediately below the spot where the television stood. And now that they all looked closely at the set they could see that water was still dripping out of it.

'But we put a bowl on it to catch the drips,' said Michael, sounding puzzled. 'It's empty. You can see for yourself.'

'You can't have put it in exactly the right place,' said Jim practically. 'Though I must say it looks big enough.'

They unplugged the set and moved it to another, drier, corner of the room to drain during the day. Then they put the bowl back on the floor, exactly where it had stood in the first place.

The next night it rained again, leaving puddles on the coffee table and the draining-board and just near Ian's bed. (He had taken the precaution of moving it a few inches.) But again the bowl was empty. 'Odd,' said Toby.

Jim the Giant arrived in the middle of breakfast. Water had entered his room again but in a new place. This time it had found its way into the jar – carelessly left open – in which he kept his iron tablets. They had turned an unsavoury orange colour. And when Jim paced the room again it was clear that the leak had sprung from directly underneath the television in its new position.

Sure enough the floor under the set was wet again and there were drips on its under-surface. The top of the set was quite dry.

'This is crazy,' Toby said. 'The set must be full of water.' They picked it up and shook it about a bit but it wasn't full of water. At least, not brim-full.

'Perhaps it runs along the aerial lead,' suggested Jim.

'But before it connects with the set,' Michael pointed out, 'the aerial lead runs uphill for a good two feet. Water, in contrast, usually doesn't do that.'

'It doesn't usually rain out of TV sets either,' Jim countered.

'Well, I'm going to talk to Mrs More,' said Toby. 'See if she knows anything about it.' And later in the morning he went to look for her.

When Toby found Mrs More she was sharing a large pot of tea with Mrs Much in the basement. They offered him a cup which he accepted and then he was taken aback to find that the tea came out of the pot – a very large one – with the milk and sugar already in it. This transplanted him so rapidly back to his schooldays that he felt his adult confidence evaporate in a matter of seconds.

'I'm sorry to trouble you,' he heard himself beginning diffidently, as though poking his head round the staff-room door, 'but there's something odd going on up on the sixth floor.' And he rather haltingly explained the whole story.

'These old houses,' said Mrs Much. 'They're all the same. T' rain goes in at one place under t' slates and

46

comes through at another.'

'It's a devil of a job to trace,' said Mrs More. 'I remember one year there were water coming down t' chimney here. They traced it back to a leak at number sixteen.'

'At number sixteen, I ask you!' said Mrs Much.

'Yes, but that isn't quite the point,' Toby persisted. 'It's precisely that there's no possible connection between the roof and the television and I can't think of any explanation...'

'Why does tha want an explanation?' Mrs More seemed to be getting cross. 'Tha's got a bowl to catch the water, hasn't tha? Why does tha need an explanation as well. If tha'd simply left the bowl where tha found it under t' set tha wouldn't have a problem. Who needs an explanation?'

'But that's ridiculous,' said Toby, the confidence of his thirty-eight years reasserting itself. 'It's quite abnormal, don't you see, to have water appearing like that. It might be a poltergeist or something.' Toby had an idea suddenly. His encounter with Natasha the publicity offer at Slimbridge had taught him a thing or two. 'We could get onto the local TV station if you like. They could run a news story on it.' He had another idea. 'You could make some money out of it.'

'Make money?' shrilled Mrs Much as if deeply offended by the idea. 'Don't be so bloody daft. Tha might as well try selling pebbles on t' beach.'

'Pebbles on t' beach, yes, that's right. Tha might as well,' echoed Mrs More. 'Nobody's made any money hereabouts since t' chimneysweep's last visit and that were a good few years ago now.'

'Proper money, now,' said Mrs More. 'We haven't seen proper money since Alf were alive.'

'Not since Wilf died.' Mrs Much swallowed a high-pitched sob.

'Even before that it weren't that much,' added Mrs More with a sob of her own.

'Not much more,' came from Mrs More painfully.

'It's a hard, hard life,' said Mrs Much.

'Hard and bitter.' Mrs More's voice rose above her sister's sobbing.

'To think of it,' Mrs Much howled. 'And tha talks of money. Money!'

'I'm sorry,' said Toby, aghast at the pitch towards which the conversation was rising. 'I only meant to talk about the water in the television. I didn't intend to…'

'What does tha know?' screeched Mrs Much.

'You people are all the same,' Mrs More went on, a ferocious semitone higher than her sister. 'You southerners. What do you know of t' north-east? You create half the problems here. Always have done. It goes back all t' way to William t' Conqueror. You come here and study t' problems. Then what do you give us? Explanations! The Domesday Book. Explanations ain't t' answer to nothing!'

'And another thing...' Mrs Much was approaching top C sharp.

Toby thought this might be an appropriate moment to bring the discussion to an end. 'Well, thanks most awfully for the tea,' he said, getting up awkwardly from the table. 'See you later.' And he backed out of the room.

'Well, what did she say?' the others asked him a few minutes later.

'Well,' he began once he had recaptured his breath from the six flights of stairs. 'Mrs Much was there too. We had a cup of tea...'

'But what did they say?' Michael repeated.

'They said that life was hard and that making money was even harder.'

'But what about the water?'

'They intimated that it was a regional issue and that outsiders weren't qualified to judge it. Apparently it only appears odd to us because we don't understand the north-east. Anyway, as far as they're concerned the matter is closed.'

'Have you gone mad?' asked Michael. 'Or are they crazy and it's catching? A regional issue? I never heard such rubbish!' His astonishment then reduced him to silence.

'They may be right,' said Ian reflectively. He told them the story of the tailor's dummies and the firemen. 'If a child can see corpses being chucked into the street and find it quite normal that they're left lying there, why can't we see water gushing from a television set and think that normal too? It's all a matter of adjusting your perceptions. The North-East is different. Those two old bats are right.'

Michael shook his head in disbelief but Toby went without a word and put the bowl back under the television where it had been in the first place.

That night Toby listened to the rain crashing onto the slates as he lay in bed. He heard the wind baying along the beach and shifting the pebbles for no money at all and he saw the darkness pressing against the little window like something solid and powerful trying to get in. He thought about the following week, which was to be spent somewhere in the Midlands and began to look forward to the end of the current week with a sense of urgency. Then he slept.

When morning broke it brought with it the thin but promising sunshine of early March. One by one Toby and Michael and Ian approached the bowl beneath the television set and peered into it. It was full of water. To their surprise – and especially to Michael's – this discovery filled them with real pleasure, topping up what had already been provided by the morning sunshine. They emptied the bowl with a great sense of achievement and invited Jim the Giant upstairs for breakfast by way of celebration.

It was later that day that Toby and Michael noticed that number sixteen – whose leaking roof had produced water in the chimney of number twenty-seven, according to Mrs More – was actually on the other side of the road. It was then that they stopped struggling against the North-East and decided to like it. After all, as Ian said to them a little later on that day, 'The North-East is another country. It rains differently there.'

Collingtree Mansions

Sometimes actors on tour can go home for the weekend like normal people. Sometimes they can't. It depends how far the next date is from London. London is home, of course, because, though it is no longer a handicap to a young actor to have a regional accent, a regional address in quite another matter. An accent from Piddletrenthide in deepest Dorset, for example, would do you no harm – might even help to make you a star – but a home address there would make you a non-starter. (Paradoxically the reverse would become true once your stardom became an accomplished fact.)

Ian took the night train down from the north-eastern Tyne and Wear coast, arriving in time for breakfast at King's Cross – where there wasn't any. Then he went by underground to Notting Hill Gate and walked up the Portobello Road to Collingtree Mansions where he had a room and a slice of kitchen at number 9c.

Under the portico which shaded six litter-strewn steps from the lemony sunshine sat a dark-complexioned lady with a mop of carrot-coloured hair. 'Good morning,' said Ian.

'Good morning,' said the lady.

Ian went into the grimy hallway where a fleet of bicycles lay at anchor and climbed two huge flights of graffiti-ed stone stairs. Then he turned his key in the lock of a big door and, putting the brutish world of the communal stairs firmly on the other side of it, entered a peaceful Edwardian apartment where only the threadbare state of the patterned carpet and the chipped veneer of the dark massive furniture suggested the passing of most of the twentieth century. From behind a closed door came the authoritative sound of Bach being played on a big piano.

'Hello.' A warm elderly voice approached along the corridor. 'We haven't seen you for weeks. Would you like some porridge?'

'Oh hello, Marta. No thank you. But I'd love a...'

'There's one in the pot. Come into the kitchen.'

'Thank you,' said Ian. 'But why is Mrs Mahooda sitting on the steps with her hair looking like a dish of grated carrot?' They had drifted into the kitchen. Ian sat at the table and Marta poured tea.

'Her husband left her on Tuesday. She had the hair-do on Wednesday in order to bring him back and she's been sitting out there ever since so he can see her if he's passing.'

'What, day and night?'

'She comes in in the evening to feed the children but she's out there all day. Miss Toil takes her cups of tea from time to time.'

'Miss Toil does?' Miss Toil lived by herself on the ground floor. Ian thought she was about a hundred and twenty.

'Yes, it's given her quite a new lease of life, having someone permanently outside her front window.'

'I didn't know Miss Toil ever spoke to Mrs Mahooda.'

'Well, she didn't for years but this seems to have brought them together. It's an ill wind...'

'I don't know that if I were Mr Mahooda I would be tempted back by a hair-do. Especially that colour.'

'Ah, but Ian, just think. You're not Mr Mahooda. Someone like you might not have left her in the first place.'

'That's what I might not have done in the second place,' said Ian. 'In the first place I might not have married her. Any other news?'

'Paul's learning Bach's second Partita on the piano. He broke his first string last week – though that was in Brahms of course. He was very proud of himself. He said it showed how his dynamic range was being extended.'

'It's always sounded pretty extended to me,' said Ian. 'Especially when I'm trying to have a lie-in in the morning.'

'Alice is back in the typing pool,' Marta continued with the news bulletin. 'She's had auditions but nothing's worked out for her lately. Sometimes I think if she wasn't such a good secretary she might have a better chance as an actress. It's something in the face I always think. Mike Pike seems to be on the brink of a new job but he'll tell you all about that himself when he gets up. He's here this weekend.'

'And Max?'

'Max is just the same. He's officially left the Communist Party and joined the Greens. It makes shopping so much more difficult. It was his birthday last week. I made a green cake. No candles, of course, because of the greenhouse effect. In any case he doesn't like to remember how old he's getting.'

'How old is he getting?'

'Since last week, seventy-seven. Anyway, it's not at all easy, a green cake. If you do it properly, that is. All eggs from hens that are certified free-range going back three generations. Flour from wheat that hasn't suffered harvest shock...'

'Harvest shock? What's that?'

'It's the chemical change caused to the cells of plants at the moment when we kill them in order to eat them. Apparently it reduces the dignity of their deaths and impairs the flavour... And then, after all that he wouldn't eat the icing because he'd heard a radio programme about working conditions in the sugar-beet industry. I thought that one of the advantages of being Green was that you didn't have to worry about people any more. But apparently not.'

'The radio certainly does have a lot to answer for,' said Ian. 'Have you thought of taking it away from him? Anyway, did he get up for his birthday this year?'

'No, he celebrated it in bed as usual. He did get up for Christmas, if you remember. Maybe he'll manage the birthday as well next year. Rome wasn't built in a day. At least he keeps himself busy.'

'Doing what?'

'He's memorising the tragedies of Shakespeare,' said Marta with a beaming smile.

'What? All of them?'

'Well, he intends to. He says the Tragedies cheer him up. Learning them makes him feel more positive about life. He's got Hamlet off by heart already. Now he's making a start on King Lear.'

Bach's second Partita came to an abrupt stop at that point and seconds later Paul was in the kitchen. 'Have some tea,' said Marta.

'Love some,' said Paul. 'I suppose there isn't any porridge left?'

Marta had realised long ago that young people who worked in the arts were always hungry and so, because she was a generous landlady – although not a rich one – there was always porridge around somewhere, and tea and coffee, and old-fashioned biscuits that crumbled in the hand and fell on the floor and thus – as was fitting in such a kind-hearted establishment as Marta's – helped also to keep an unknown number of families of mice from hunger and destitution.

'Hello stranger,' said Paul to Ian. 'Welcome back. How's the tour going?'

'Well, it's my first one, so it's difficult to compare. It seems to be making a massive loss wherever it goes – except for one place where the publicity lady sold it on the strength of a newspaper photo of some female legs sticking out of the building's windows... And we've met some weird people. An alcoholic landlady – and a posh hostess who'd failed to notice a cow that had fallen into her swimming-pool and got frozen into the ice... Probably pretty average, I'd guess.'

'Have you managed to go on yet?' Paul asked, remembering that Ian was an understudy as well as an ASM.'

'No. No one's been ill yet, unfortunately.'

'They will be,' said Paul reassuringly. 'Be patient. All good things come to those who wait.'

'Thank you. The Bach sounds good.'

'Does it? Thank you. It's a bugger to learn, though. (Sorry Marta.) Anyway, I'd better crack on. Thanks for the porridge.' Paul got up and disappeared along the corridor.

'He works so hard,' said Marta, shaking her head

wistfully, as the reverberant boom and chime of the Bechstein grand started up again behind the closed door of the music room.

'And here comes someone who doesn't,' said Ian as Mike Pike, who was roughly the same age as Paul and Ian, peered round the door, clad only in a towel.

'Morning Marta. Nice to see you back, Ian.'

'What's this about a job, Mike?'

'Tell you in the pub. Can't stop now. Appointment with some bathwater. Twelve o'clock, though, in The Alexandra.'

'Actually,' said Mike at two minutes past twelve, once he'd taken his first long mouthful of Directors' bitter, 'the new job's with your lot.'

'You're joining the Gulliver tour?!' Ian's voice showed his astonishment.

'No,' said Mike. 'Not with Gulliver. But it is with Nathan McCaffrey. You know he's got this big show coming up – Yes We Have No Pyjamas?'

'Yes, of course. You don't mean you've landed a part in it?'

'Yes I do. Well, yes and no. I mean it's like your job. ASM understudy. Only of course it'll be West End money. Just two weeks Out Of Town and then *In*.'

'In,' echoed Ian wistfully, enviously.

'Yes. It's definite. And also I get to appear.'

'You go on? That's great,' said Ian.

Mike pulled a bit of a face. 'Well, I don't exactly go on. I do come off, though.'

'Without going on?'

'Well actually I'm dragged off. When the curtain goes up there's this corpse on stage. Well lit, you understand, and downstage centre, but two men drag me offstage right away, before anything else begins to happen.'

'Wow,' said Ian, very impressed. 'Good costume and make-up? Lots of blood and guts?'

'No, that's the sad thing. I'm face-down.'

'Never mind,' said Ian. 'It's a great start. 'When do you go into rehearsal?'

'Tomorrow week,' said Mike.

'Well congratulations,' Ian said magnanimously. Their relationship, though friendly, had always been mildly competitive – ever since they'd played Rosencrantz and Guildenstern together at drama school and had had trouble remembering which of them was supposed to be which. 'But is Yes We Have No Pyjamas all cast?'

'Yes.'

'Even Binky?'

'Especially Binky. It's the main part.'

'Oh God,' said Ian. 'Susan's going to be really upset when she hears.'

'Who's Susan?'

'Our leading lady. You can't miss her: she's about two miles high. But she's under the impression that Nathan promised Binky to her. Keeps going on about it.'

'Then it's time she got to know Nathan a bit better. I can tell you – strictly between ourselves – that he's promised me the lead in his next musical.'

'He's what?' said Ian, astonished and unsure whether the other thing he was feeling was jealousy or admiration.

'Yes but… That was last week. He said I had the right looks and he knows I play the piano a bit…'

'The subject of the musical being…?'

'Paganini,' said Mike smugly.

'Paganini? Can you play the violin?'

'Unfortunately not. Not a note. Not a scrape. Not a whimper.'

'Then why on earth did he want you for the part?' Ian asked. 'Even if you started to take lessons now it might be a long time before you could play like Paganini.'

'He thought Paganini was a pianist. Not that I'd have been able to play the piano like Paganini would have done if he had been a pianist... Anyway, he apologised afterwards. He said he was on the lookout for a vehicle for me. That something'd come along that I'd be just right for.'

'And you believe him when he says all this?'

'Of course not,' said Mike Pike, laughing. 'Not a bloody word. And neither should your two-mile-high Susan.'

Ian sighed. 'I suppose I'll have to break it to her. But I'm glad you're not swallowing his promises...'

Mike gave a quiet smile that Ian thought a bit enigmatic. 'On the other hand, I think I know a way of making things come true if I want to...'

'Meaning?'

'The part of Binky's gone to this girl called Marian. Well apparently...' Mike allowed an eloquent facial expression to finish the sentence for him. He had an extensive repertoire of eloquent facial expressions.

'Surely you wouldn't!' said Ian, horrified. 'Anyway, Marian's a girl. And Nathan...'

'Don't be too sure. Rumour has it that when he was younger...' He provided another eloquent facial expression to complete the sentence.

'But you wouldn't, would you?' Ian was shocked in spite of himself. 'I mean, with Nathan…?'

This time Mike's facial expression provided the whole of his answer.

'Mike! You sly, cynical, two-edged little…'

'Spare me the final compliment and I'll buy you the next pint. It'll be a pleasure to, now I know I'm going to have money coming in … as from Monday week.'

'Would you like me to lend you some till then?' asked Ian.

Mike smiled broadly. 'Well, a fiver wouldn't half be welcome.' The smile broadened even further. 'Then I could buy you another beer this evening.'

On the way back they saw that Mrs Mahooda was still sitting on the steps. Sitting next to her was Miss Toil in a sun bonnet. They were sharing a half-bottle of tonic wine.

The next morning Marta called to Ian just as he was leaving for the station. 'I'm sure you'll be pleased to know that Mr Mahooda came back last night. Now all is peace and love between them.'

'Good heavens,' said Ian. 'Was it the hair-do?'

'Apparently not,' said Marta. 'Miss Toil lent Mrs Mahooda an old sun bonnet with a bunch of cherries on the rim of it. And the cherries clinched it.'

The Man Who Was Thursday

'Can you do without me during the daytime on Friday?' Philip the stage manager asked Nick. (Nick was the company manager. Remember? Philip's immediate boss.)

'I daresay we'll manage,' said Nick. 'What's on?'

'I've got an interview.'

'Where?'

'At the BBC. Production assistant. With a man whose name you won't forget in a hurry. Peter Thursday-Valentine.'

'I know him,' said Nick. 'Met him at least. He interviewed me for a job a couple of years back. I didn't get it.'

'Why not?' asked Philip.

'I looked at his hair,' said Nick.

'You did what?'

'He wears a toupee, hairpiece, wig, whatever. It's not so bad that you spot it at once, but it's not so good as to be able to escape detection in the long term. Once I'd begun to suspect his hair wasn't all his own it became difficult to take my eyes off it. At first I glanced at it quickly every time he looked away. Then I found my eyes wandering up to it even when he was looking directly at me. By the time twenty minutes were up so were my chances of getting the job. He asked me a few more questions but with less and less enthusiasm. Then he stood up, thanked me for coming and said he'd be in touch. I knew by then that I'd blown it.'

'Bad luck,' said Philip. 'Still, thanks for the tip-off. I'll remember not to look above his eyebrows. And I'll be back by five o'clock at the latest.'

Philip arrived at the BBC in good time, took the lift to the correct floor and was shown into an armchair which had a potted rubber plant on one side of it and a plinth ashtray on the other. 'Mr Thursday-Valentine won't keep you long,' said his receptionist. 'But he's running a bit behind with his yoga. There's some back numbers of The Radio Times you can look at if you like.'

The receptionist disappeared and Philip was soon engrossed in the exploits of Captain Pugwash. When the cartoons had first appeared in the Radio Times he had been a bit young for them but now he found he could understand them better. He was just getting into the story where the barrel of black pepper is switched for one of gunpowder when the corner of his eye was caught by something else.

A cloud of smoke was rising from the ashtray by his side, and not from a lonely cigarette-end on the top but from the bottom of the well charged interior of the plinth. It struck Philip first that here was an obvious chance to prove his mettle as a man of action and, therefore, an excellent production assistant and, secondly, that the situation might well be a put-up one – that it was part of the selection process in fact – and that whether he got the job or not probably depended on his response to it. He walked coolly over to the receptionist's desk. 'Do you think I could have a glass of water?' he asked.

'I'm sorry,' said the receptionist. 'You'd need to go to the canteen for that. But don't worry. Mr Thursday-Valentine's still five minutes from finishing his exercises.'

'In that case,' said Philip, 'is there a fire extinguisher handy?'

The receptionist looked at him oddly. 'That's some thirst,' she said. 'But if you're really desperate I've got a can of Coke in my handbag.'

'Perfect,' said Philip. 'But quickly.'

The receptionist handed him the can, then watched in wonder as he disappeared behind the rubber plant and disposed of the can's contents with a hissing sound. Philip re-emerged from behind the plant pot beaming a triumphant smile and wreathed in clouds of smoke and steam that gave him an even stronger resemblance to Mephistopheles than was usual.

'What the hell...?' A door had opened behind the reception desk and Mr Thursday-Valentine stood framed in the opening.

'I'm Philip.' Smoke and steam continued to billow around him. 'About the post of assistant?'

Peter Thursday-Valentine turned out to be a charming, kindly man. You could imagine he had been very good-looking once. He was a good interviewer, having the knack of putting people at their ease and then firing off a deadly question when they were least expecting it. But Philip hardly noticed any of this. What claimed the whole of his attention was that Thursday-Valentine had BBC length hair of a distinguished iron-grey colour which swept back from a noble if receding forehead and which nearly but not quite concealed a balding patch of the size that, on a man of his seniority, you might expect.

If this is a toupee, thought Philip, it's an extremely good one. No wonder Nick couldn't keep his eyes off it. What a masterstroke of subtlety to have incorporated into the design a bald patch in the middle and a receding hairline at the front.

Mr Thursday-Valentine asked Philip about his experience as a touring stage manager. Philip replied, looking at the floor. He asked him about his background in regional rep. Philip focused his gaze on a standard lamp. Thursday-Valentine talked about petty cash systems and monthly audits. Philip pressed the tips of his fingers together and answered, studying his shoes. In a low conspiratorial tone Thursday-Valentine talked of problems with the Unions. Philip responded in similar tones while staring at a Picasso reproduction on the wall.

At last Mr Peter Thursday-Valentine rose to his feet. He was impressed, he said. He needed to discuss Philip with one or two other people, but it was fairly certain that he would be joining the team. Detailed information and a contract would then be sent to him by post.

Never had an interview gone so well for Philip. He burbled his thanks. Then, with a laugh in his voice and as winsomely as only Philip knew how to be, he said, 'May I say, if I'm not being too personal, what a magnificent toupee you're wearing. I've never seen such a sophisticated one in my life.'

The temperature in the room dropped. Philip failed to notice that. 'I'm sorry?' said Mr Thursday-Valentine.

'Your wig,' said Philip. 'People say they can spot it but they're quite wrong. Believe me, it's marvellous.'

'I don't wear a toupee,' said Thursday-Valentine, his voice turning from wine to vinegar, only more quickly.

'Of course you've every right to say that,' said Philip. 'But it really is extraordinarily subtle. So good.'

There was a second's silence. Then Mr Thursday-Valentine said, 'What the eff are you talking about?' This was the BBC after all.

'Your wig,' said Philip, smiling. 'It's just so good.'

'I've told you twice,' said Mr Thursday-Valentine. 'If

necessary I'll make that three. I'm not wearing a wig of any sort. Now thank you but I have other people to see.' He indicated the door. 'Jennifer will show you out.' It occurred to Philip as Jennifer did so that he might not be receiving a contract in the post after all.

'I've been thinking,' said Nick when Philip arrived back in the stage management office on the stroke of five o'clock. 'You were wrong about this producer chap. His name isn't Thursday-Valentine, it's Tuesday-Valentine. I hope you didn't call him by the wrong name. You know how particular these BBC types can be. Unless of course…' the idea made Nick smile '…unless there are two of them. A Peter Tuesday-Valentine and a Peter Thursday-Valentine… Maybe they've got one for every day of the week. I wonder if they all wear toupees.'

'I can't speak for the others,' said Philip, 'but the man who interviewed me was Thursday-Valentine. And he doesn't wear a wig.'

'How can you be sure of that?' asked Nick.

'He told me,' Philip said.

Correspondence

Nathan was delighted to find that the empty cigarette packet in the pot-pourri bowl had been replaced by a full one. He helped himself to two cigarettes – one for later. Then he returned to the Lamb room to compose, in the steely breakfast-time light, the following letter.

Darling Susan

I am very sorry not to have written before: not to have been in touch before being (deservedly) cut to the quick by your letter. The fault is mine, of course, and on so many counts. First, in that I have managed things so wretchedly as to promise you in good faith a part which was to overlap in its timing with my previous gift to you – namely, the role of Glumdalclitch in Gulliver's Travels, wherein you are as superb as ever, if not even more radiant with the passage of time…

He crossed out 'wherein' and wrote 'in which'.

Secondly, insofar as…

The telephone rang and Nathan picked it up. 'Who is

it?' he barked. It was the company manager from Yes We Have No Pyjamas with a problem. 'I see,' said Nathan after listening to the problem for twelve seconds. 'Well, you have carte blanche, you know … Tell them I said so … to take any action you see fit – so long as it doesn't cost any money. 'Bye now.' He put the phone down and picked up his fountain pen again.

…Secondly, insofar as I should have let you know straight away when I made my decision about the casting of Binky, however painful that would have been for both of us, instead of letting you find out in such a round-the-corner fashion…

He paused. Round the corner didn't look quite right. Then he reflected that he didn't actually know how she had found out (somebody in the Gulliver company must know somebody in the Pyjamas company – but who?), so he crossed the words out and made the sentence end: *in such a fashion.*

…Thirdly…

He thought a bit but couldn't remember a third thing to apologise for and concluded after a while that there probably wasn't one. So he crossed out 'thirdly' and, going back to the beginning of the letter, altered 'on so many counts' to 'on two counts'. Then he went on:

...I can only plead in extenuation that I have been unprecedentedly busy with a whole multitude of ephemera connected with Gulliver, and with Yes We Have No Pyjamas, and ongoing plans for the future into which (I need hardly say) you are inextricably woven in my mind. For example, I have in mind a musical version of The Prophecies of Nostradamus in which there would be a whole string of parts just crying out for your special gifts. I also have a plan afoot to do a marathon production of all the major literary masterpieces of the last ten years performed end-to-end in a blockbusting five and a half hours.

So you may see that, if pressure of work has prevented me from time to time from keeping you abreast of a few immediate details, you are never really far from the forefront of my mind or from the wishes of my heart.

Let me now, in a woefully inadequate attempt to make up for earlier lapses, be the first to tell you that, thanks to continuing and unflagging interest in Gulliver especially since its spectacular success at Slimbridge. I am able to announce a string of new dates right up to the middle of May and an extension of everyone's contract accordingly.

But rather than end with this smallish crumb of comfort I beg you to think about the longer term, and of our greater and more profitable partnerships in the future.

Thinking of you as I always do,

With Love

Nathan

He laid the draft on Bunjy's desk and turned his attention to other matters. In particular, to how he could manage to stall the payment of his outstanding debt to Moses the Wigmakers for even longer.

When Bunjy drew his attention to the arrival of the morning's post an hour later she mentioned in particular a letter that had come from Susan.

'Yes, I know,' he said. 'I was expecting it. You needn't bother to open it. I've answered it already. My draft's on your desk. An especially good letter, I can't help thinking.'

'And the letter from Susan?' Bunjy queried, although she already knew the answer.

'File it with the others.'

So the whole postbag went into the bin as usual, once Bunjy had run her eye over the most important items and removed the cheques – as well as peeling with a well-practised thumbnail the stamps from the many reply-hopeful self-addressed envelopes from desperate actors.

Whiplash and Sea-lions

As a result of two consecutive dates that were in easy reach of London – if a little liable to mix-up, being Weybridge and Woodbridge – Ian found himself back at Collingtree Mansions just a fortnight after his last visit. He was delighted to have the five pounds that he had lent to Mike Pike returned to him on Saturday morning (Mike was by now on salary as the acting ASM on Yes We Have No Pyjamas) and to find that Mike didn't immediately ask to borrow it back again on the Sunday evening – as had often happened in the past – in The Alexandra.

Ian also took the opportunity to pick up a pair of contact lenses for which he had previously been measured from Dolland and Aitchison at Notting Hill Gate, before setting off on Monday afternoon for Woodbridge. Or Weybridge...

Actually it was Weybridge, Ian remembered just in time before he bought his ticket at the station. Woodbridge had been last week.

Not everyone took digs in Weybridge. Some of the company who lived in the southern suburbs chose to commute instead. Susan and Peter in particular, as owners of their own cars. But Ian once again found himself under the same roof as Toby and Michael, this time as the paying guest of a Mrs Honey. 'I think she's another one of those,' said Michael with a significant look on his face when they first met her.

When they met her again, late on Monday night, there was no doubt about it. 'I hadn't realised there were four of you,' she said mildly. 'I was sure you were only going to be three.'

'We are only three,' they all said.

'But I distinctly see four of you,' said Mrs Honey. 'Well, fairly distinctly.'

'We promise we're only three, honestly,' said Toby.

'Scout's honour,' offered Michael.

'Cross our hearts and hope to die,' appealed Ian.

'It still looks like four of you,' said Mrs Honey.

'We must convince her somehow,' whispered Michael to Toby 'She'll want to charge us for four otherwise.'

'Look,' said Toby to Mrs Honey, 'We'll go out again and come in slowly, one at a time. You count very carefully and you'll see only three. Promise.'

'Cross my...' began Ian but the others pushed him out of the door.

'Well,' said Mrs Honey when the exercise was complete, 'it's most peculiar. It's true that I only counted up to three and yet here you are, four again. I really don't understand it. Perhaps the back door...'

'Perhaps you're tired, Mrs Honey,' said Michael gently. 'Maybe if we all went to bed now it would be easier to sort out in the morning.'

And happily, Mrs Honey agreed.

But in the morning there were four places laid for breakfast. Mrs Honey was at a loss to understand how the fourth man had got away unobserved by her, because she always got up very early herself. This was so that she could put her empty bottles in the dustbin before the neighbours were awake. She liked to wrap them in newspaper – the bottles, not the neighbours – to stop them chinking together in a tell-tale, bottle-like way.

Luckily, on Tuesday night she only saw three and a half of them and by Wednesday they were down to a more satisfactory whole number. On Thursday morning only three plates were laid for breakfast and when the bill was finally presented to them on Saturday it was for three people only; the fourth man seemed to be completely forgotten. But by Saturday a lot else had happened.

It was during breakfast on Thursday that the phone rang and was for Ian.

'No!' the others heard him say. 'Is she all right?' And then, 'Sea-lions? Did you say sea-lions?' Then, 'Yes, I'll tell them. OK. I'll be right there.' He hung up.

'Problems?' asked Toby through toast and

marmalade.

'You bet. That was Nick. Susan's in hospital. With concussion. She's had a car smash. I think she ran over a sea-lion.'

'Ran over a sea-lion?' queried Toby.

'I think that's what Nick said. Anyway, I've got to get over to the theatre right away and there's to be an emergency meeting of the whole company at eleven.'

'Who'll play Glumdalclitch?' wondered Michael aloud.

'God knows,' said Ian. 'Anyway, see you later.'

'We'll be over in half an hour or so,' said Toby. 'See if there's anything we can do.'

'Thanks,' said Ian and off he went.

'That sounded like rather bad news,' said Mrs Honey, arriving with a fresh pot of coffee. 'I'm sorry if you're having problems with your sea-lion. Would you like a small sherry? Take your mind off it for a bit?'

'No thank you,' said Toby.

'No thanks,' said Michael.

'Well I hope you don't mind if I have another. It's beginning to be quite a morning.'

Urgent discussions were already in progress among the stage management when Michael and Toby arrived in the spare dressing-room that was earmarked as Nick's office for the week. 'The wreath's in hand,' Philip was saying, ticking it off on a list. 'I've seen to that myself.'

'You don't call it a wreath, you idiot,' said Nick. 'Not if the person's still alive. You just call it sending flowers. You didn't actually order a wreath, did you?'

'Well actually…'

'Oh my God!' said Nick.

'Cheer up, Nick,' said Michael. 'With any luck she may have popped her clogs by the time it gets there.'

'That isn't funny.'

'What about this seal?' Toby asked.

'Sea-lion,' corrected Nick. 'And it was two of them. One was killed, the other's suffering from shock.'

'Are we sending fish?' asked Michael.

'That isn't funny either,' said Nick.

'I still don't understand,' Toby persisted, 'how she came to run over a sea-lion in the first place.'

'She didn't run over it. She ran into a circus van at traffic lights on her way home last night. She got very bad whiplash and one of the sea-lions was catapulted out of its tank into the Finchley Road. It affected Susan quite badly. Apparently she spent the first part of the night under the impression that she was a sea-lion but they poured a bucket of cold water over her and she quickly realised that she wasn't. However, that brings us back to the fact that she won't be working again for a good few days yet and I've got the job of deciding how we cope in the meantime. Nathan's given me carte blanche to act as I think fit and he'll stand by whatever decision I make.'

'So long as it doesn't cost any money,' said Toby, who had had many years' experience of Nathan. Since those had in fact been Nathan's exact words Nick could only glare at Toby in reply.

'I've decided,' Nick resumed, 'having looked at all the possible permutations, that Ian will have to play Flimnapp and Jim the Giant must shave his beard off and have a crack at Glumdalclitch.'

'Jim won't,' said Toby. 'You'd never dare suggest that if he was here, so let's not waste time. You might as well ask Peter to do it.'

'Look,' said Nick. 'Who's company manager here, me or you?'

'Shut up, Nick,' everyone else told him.

'There is no alternative,' said Michael suddenly. 'Ian will have to play Glumdalclitch.'

'Oh for God's sake, Michael,' said Ian in some alarm. 'It says ASM and Understudy in my contract, but only the bloody male parts. I've never played a female in my life. I'd be totally unconvincing as a girl.'

'Then it's time you learnt,' said Michael.

'Now don't worry,' said Toby reassuringly. 'Try to think of the character as a very small giant who happens, just happens mind, to be a female. Have you ever been the back of a pantomime horse?'

'Well, no,' said Ian, frowning, 'not actually.'

'Well, when you are, you don't worry about what sex the animal is; you just get in and do it.'

Ian thought for a moment. He'd been regretting the continuing good health of the company for weeks. And now at long last someone had happily met with an accident. He could hardly let himself be seen to flinch when the moment came. But the dire possibility of making his professional debut as a juvenile giantess had never for a second entered his calculations.

'Well, Ian?' Nick broke the silence, happy that the next difficult decision lay, at least for the moment, with someone else.

'All right,' said the ASM understudy and trainee drag-artist in a voice of defeat. 'Will somebody please show me how to do the make-up?'

'There's another problem,' said Nick wearily, in the voice of one who is only four seventeenths of the way down a long list. 'The costumes will need altering. Now I gather the resident wardrobe mistress has her day off

on a Thursday. Her assistant comes in after lunch but –
unfortunately – she can't touch buttons.'

'Can't touch buttons?' queried Fran. 'What on earth is
she doing in wardrobe?'

'Apparently one frightened her when she was little,'
said Philip. 'Working here is part of her therapy.'

'And she gets paid for this?' said Michael.

'No,' said Nick. 'She's here on the National Health.'

'Velcro,' said Fran decisively and Philip wrote the
word down.

Ian emerged at that point from an ashen-faced two
minutes' silence. 'There's no way I could sing those
songs. It's ten years since I was a soprano. They'll have
to be cut.'

'It would be very difficult to get that done at such
short notice,' said Philip. 'And also expensive. One
would have to go private, and I imagine the doctors
round here…'

'The songs, you idiot,' said Ian, beginning to lose his
cool in his growing panic. 'I mean the songs will have to
be cut.'

Nick reasserted himself with a bit of an effort. 'I've
already thought about that,' he said. 'Fran will sing, *You
Can't Make an Omelette without Breaking Eggs,* but *If
The Man-Mountain Won't Come to Mildendo* will have
to go. Edward will just have to busk a few bars to cover

the scene change.' Philip made a note of this.

'Well, if there's anything else we can do...' said Michael. 'You'll find us in the Dolphin.' And there in due course everybody did.

By the time Ian had received the kind advice of all sixteen other members of the Gulliver company he was feeling about as confident and self-assured as a parachutist whose parachute still hasn't opened after the sixteenth tug on the rip-cord. But in one of the traditions that the acting profession shared with the Red Berets he was doing his best not to show it.

'I know it's not that big a part,' he said to them all. 'I mean, compared to Hamlet. But it is the female lead after all. And then there's all the other scenes. Susan had bits and pieces. Fifteen parts she had – er – has. And eight costumes. Most of which had to be worn inside out as well in order to cover the fifteen roles. I'm terrified of putting on the wrong frock, or putting it on the wrong way round, for the wrong scene.'

'Just remember the lines and don't fall over the furniture,' they all said.

'But that's just it. I might easily fall over the furniture. It's these new contact lenses: I'm still getting used to them.'

'Don't worry,' they all said.

'I feel sick,' said Ian.

'Doctor Footlights will soon take care of that,' they said.

'Can nerves make you lose your voice?' Ian asked the others anxiously.

'No,' said Fran.

'Yes,' said Peter.

'Have a Scotch before you go on,' said Toby.

'Honey and lemon,' said Edward.

'Port and brandy,' said Michael.

'Runny ice-cream,' said Jim the Giant.

'Yuk,' said Ian.

The afternoon rehearsal passed all too quickly for Ian. While it was going on the wardrobe assistant who couldn't touch buttons altered the costumes with the help of the Gulliver wardrobe mistress, Linda, who could. They shortened the Glumdalclitch costume – for though Ian was tallish he was no match for Susan – and Linda re-positioned the buttons with a little help from Philip. There was no time for any tea, but Ian didn't feel hungry anyway. He was in the middle of doing his make-up, with some help and encouragement from Michael, when the door of his dressing-room was flung open after the shortest of unanswered knocks and there, complete with silk scarf, gold watch-chain and silver-knobbed cane, stood Nathan McCaffrey. Nathan, who never left London except to avoid his wife, Nathan who hadn't seen Gulliver since its first night back in November …Nathan had come all the way to Weybridge and was now in the room.

'I've come to see you knock 'em for six, Ian,' Nathan barked. He looked around the dressing-room that all seven of the male actors shared. 'I expect everyone to knock 'em for six. I've come in the expectation of a memorable show. Woe betide anyone who lets me down.' He stretched out a hand and placed it on Ian's shoulder before saying, a little less fiercely, 'Well, break a leg, old boy. There'll be a drink on me in the bar afterwards.' Then, while he was there he whispered very quietly in Ian's ear, 'And if you can find out who it was that let Susan know she hadn't got the part of Binky in No Pyjamas I'd be delighted to hear from you.' Then he whirled round and was gone.

'Well, well, well,' said Michael, who hadn't heard what Nathan had whispered in Ian's ear. 'There's a surprise. They say the last time he bought a round was on the opening night of The Mousetrap.' Ian didn't manage to reply. He had the impression that his legs were turning to jelly, beginning at the knees.

Nathan Makes History

Nathan kept his promise. There was a drink for everyone in the bar after the show, the first round he had bought in over forty glorious years. But when the curtain had come down a few minutes earlier it was widely believed that the offer would not materialise. Indeed it was a near-run thing that it did.

Nathan had watched the start of the show from the back of the stalls. The curtain had risen on time at seven thirty. At seven thirty-two Nathan had been heard to mutter, 'Oh no!' under his breath. At seven forty-one he had murmured, 'Hell.' At seven forty-eight it had been, 'Hell's Teeth!' At one minute to eight he said, 'Jesus Christ!' and moved up to the back of the circle. From there he watched the second act, during which (at eight seven, eight sixteen and eight twenty-three) he said three things which the circle usherettes, when comparing notes later with their sisters in the stalls, could not bring themselves to repeat.

During the interval Nathan overheard a furious member of the audience telling one of the bar staff that it was the worst performance of the worst production of the most ill-conceived adaptation for the stage of any work of literature that it had been his misfortune to witness. 'You should come more often,' the barman had said. 'We have this sort of thing every week.'

Nathan had wondered whether to enter the argument,

silver-headed cane whirling, watch-chain jangling, basso profundo thundering – 'Sir, I happen to be the impresario. Would you care to direct your remarks to me in person?' (Lion room tactics) or to slip quietly out of the theatre pretending to be someone else (Lamb room style). But at that moment another member of the audience had stepped up to the complaining gentleman and said quite loudly that he personally had enjoyed the show-so-far enormously. Someone else agreed with him, saying that he hadn't laughed so much since his wife had left him and then a lady in blue tights and her hair done up in a bun had said that, in her opinion, the apparently shambolic representation they had been watching was closer to the spirit of Gulliver's Travels in its anarchic randomness and wayward character than any number of more respectful adaptations or technically sound performances. She felt the production deserved a niche in British Literature in its own right, as well as an assured place in theatre history.

A London theatre critic (who just happened to be in the theatre that night with an elderly aunt who lived in Weybridge and whose birthday treat this was) took out a note-pad and wrote the blue-stockinged woman's statement down verbatim, as he had just decided that it exactly matched his own judgement of the piece and also his manner of expressing it … had he only had the opportunity to get the words out first.

Then another man said that it was clearly a show that needed to be seen a second time and that, for his part, he was going straight down to the box-office to book more tickets for the following night. Almost everyone followed him down the stairs, leaving the bar empty except for Nathan and the man who had complained about the show in the first place. 'Well, at least we've got room to breathe now,' said the latter.

Nathan didn't exactly breathe. He sort of purred. 'May I Introduce Myself. I Am Nathan McCaffrey The Impresario,' enunciating clearly all the capital letters. 'What Would You Like To Drink.'

By the time the curtain fell Nathan had persuaded his chance companion – for neither of them had returned to the auditorium after the interval – to invest six thousand pounds in Nathan's projected stage version of Gibbon's Decline and Fall of the Roman Empire. He was in a jovial mood when the company made its timid entrance into the bar a few minutes later. Amazed at this cheerfulness the cast began to sip their free drinks cautiously, like antelope at the rim of a crocodile-infested water-hole, but eventually reassuring themselves that it really was the case that Nathan was as happy as a sand-bag about something, and was not about to storm and rage or sack them on the spot, they began to talk more freely among themselves about their experiences during the last two hours.

'Why,' someone asked, 'didn't the curtain rise at the beginning of the play?'

'It's normally Ian's job,' Toby answered. 'Nobody thought to reallocate the task. And as nobody had been told to take the tabs out, nobody did. Until Nick clocked the situation a few minutes later.'

'Fantastic effect,' said Nathan, homing in on the conversation from the other side of the room. 'We're keeping it in. The sheer novelty of the first three minutes of the action taking place behind velvet curtains, unseen, half-heard, yet profoundly sensed, is breathtaking in its impact and daring.'

The London theatre critic, whom Nathan had invited (along with his elderly aunt) to stay and join the party, wrote this down.

Another pair of actors were discussing the moment in the Academy scene when the stage-flats representing an entire side wall had come crashing onto the stage, bringing with them the three members of the stage crew who, in Ian's absence, had been trying to prop them up from behind. 'Magnificent,' said Nathan, appearing from nowhere. 'We're keeping it in. The surprise element, so inextricably a part of life yet so rarely found, in its profoundest sense, in dramatic representations of it.' The critic wrote this down too.

But the biggest crowd was gathered around Ian. 'What I want to know,' Peter was asking, 'is why in God's name you played Glumdalclitch wearing spectacles? Especially your spectacles.' (Ian's were of the Trotsky sort.) 'And if you were going to wear the bloody things, why didn't you warn us first? I thought I was going to die from trying not to laugh when you came charging on. And as for the love duet … well, you heard for yourself what happened to my top B flat.' Everyone around nodded at the memory. 'Why couldn't you have worn your new contact lenses like at the rehearsal?'

'I'd taken them out to clean them,' said Ian in a penitential voice. 'Some eye-liner had got behind one of them. Then my call came and I dropped them on the floor. I didn't have any choice really. I can't see a thing without glasses, you know. I'd have fallen over the furniture and into the flats like anything. But I'm terribly sorry it made everyone laugh so much, and I really do feel bad about your top B flat.'

'Feel bad, Ian?' boomed a familiar voice suddenly at his side. 'Feel bad? Nonsense, my boy. Tonight you were wonderful. Tonight you took your first step on the long road that leads to glory. Young man, with your talent and with my ... er ... everything else, we are going to make you a star. And the spectacles... Keep them in.' He turned to Peter. 'You're not to worry about the B flat. It'll come back in a day or two, once you're used to Ian's facial fenestration.' Nathan turned and addressed the room. 'The spectacles are a masterstroke, no less. By this, the most economical of means, a profound truth is revealed. These small arrangements of glass and steel provide a metaphor for the clarity of vision and the transparent goodness of heart that are Glumdalclitch's and hers alone in the Kingdom of Brobdignagg.'

He broke off in order to spell Glumdalclitch and Brobdignagg for the benefit of the rapidly scribbling critic at his side. 'Truly are these lenses the windows into the giant-girl's tender soul.' Nathan seemed stirred by the depth of his own insight and shook his head for a moment. Then he uttered the phrase that was to go down in theatre history and which would one day earn him his place in the National Dictionary of Showbusiness Quotations. 'Barman, Another Round Of Drinks.'

Cabaret Time

That Thursday night at Weybridge transformed the fortunes of the Gulliver tour. The interval had had to be extended by several minutes while the box-office dealt with the queue of customers who were re-booking to see the show a second time. The following night the show was a sell-out.

Nathan – who had had the good grace to call on Susan in hospital before returning to London, replacing Philip's wreath with a more appropriately bright bouquet of flowers – received a phone-call from a triumphant Nick, during which the company manager read out the week's sales figures to date.

'Another blip,' said Nathan. 'Remember Slimbridge?'

'You wouldn't be saying that if you could see the box-office queue at this moment,' said Nick. 'We could easily sell a second week. The management here actually wants to bring the show back again in the summer.'

'Well, well,' said Nathan, beginning to think that perhaps this was more than just a blip after all. 'It looks as though I've got a success on your hands, Nick. Don't drop it now, though, or God help you.' Then he hung up. Gulliver, until now a Lamb room show, was now transformed in Nathan's mind into a Lion room production. The next morning he called Bunjy in, even though it was a Saturday, to move the Gulliver files and accounts from the one room to the other and, when he passed Mr Riskett on the stairs, permitted himself to launch the ghost of a smile in his direction.

The Saturday night performance was also a sell-out, and even the matinee had been full. The actors continued to be suitably astonished, while the Weybridge theatre's permanent staff seemed to be going through their work in a state of trance. Ian continued to play the part of Glumdalclitch, still in spectacles and with growing assurance, while Peter climbed his way back up to his beloved B flat, like an unhorsed rider remounting his steed in order to regain his confidence. The succession of accidents that had illuminated Thursday night's performance were now officially incorporated into the production, as per Nathan's orders, and had been rehearsed and polished to a degree that would prevent them from failing to occur to plan in the future.

It was true that the little theatre in Weybridge only had a capacity of a hundred and forty-seven and a half seats – of which sixty-eight, incidentally, were situated directly behind pillars – but even so the three full houses in a row were indicators of a change that was not merely a matter of numbers. The applause at the end of the final show on Saturday night was audible from the street outside, where people actually stopped and asked each other what was going on. For some hours the rumour ran that the theatre had been sold to make way for a boxing venue. Nothing else, it was assumed, could give rise to such an outburst of spontaneous enthusiasm in Weybridge.

Sunday brought its own surprise. Two by two, the eyes of the Gulliver company opened wide as they read through their Sunday papers. Their jaws dropped open, they made incoherent noises, they ran to their telephones to contact each other, wanting to reassure themselves that what they had just read was not a dream. And it was not. Under a headline that was almost too complimentary to be published in a family newspaper the critic whose elderly aunt lived in Weybridge had written up his discovery of the Gulliver tour in the glowing terms he had first heard from the mouths of the lady with the bun and blue tights and Nathan McCaffrey.

It won't be necessary to quote his article here. Enough to say that he praised the adaptation, the music, the direction and the acting, that he mentioned Ian's name six times and that he listed the next five dates on the tour's itinerary and told his readers – a large and loyal following – that they simply had to go and see it if it came anywhere within fifty miles of where they now sat reading their Sunday papers.

When Nathan read this he got up from his chair without a word and disappeared into the cupboard under his kitchen stairs. When he came out he was holding a bottle of champagne. 'My dear,' said Mrs McCaffrey, 'do you think it is correct to drink champagne at ten o'clock on a Sunday morning? People haven't even gone to church yet.'

'One might have to wait a long time for that to happen these days,' said Nathan. 'And today of all days, yes. Have a look at this.' He thrust the newspaper review under his wife's nose.

Mrs McCaffrey raised her eyebrows. 'I see,' she said. 'In the circumstances…' She allowed Nathan to pour her a glass.

Wadebridge in Cornwall is not especially close to Weybridge, Surrey, but on the other hand it was not too difficult for a Lion room show to get to, and on this occasion the Gulliver company reached their new destination with no more than two changes of trains. A personal message was awaiting each member of the company when they arrived at the theatre. It was an invitation to dinner after the show. It was – wrote Nathan, for the author of the invitations was none other than he – by way of being a big thank you to everyone for the spectacular success of the tour so far. Unfortunately he could not join them in person, he wrote, but he had made all the arrangements and they were all to enjoy themselves as liberally as they liked at his expense.

'Isn't this amazing?' said Philip, a Mephistophelean grin wreathing its way around his features. 'First two drinks in one evening and now this. A whole, real live dinner.'

'Hmm,' said Toby, his mouth turning down at the corners a little. He added, for he had had a classical education, 'I fear Nathan, especially when he brings gifts.'

Nathan had booked them into a restaurant called The Giant's Castle and had laid on taxis to take everyone there. The taxis were welcome… The Giant's Castle was twelve miles away. It really was a castle, with moat and drawbridge, set in the depths of the Cornish countryside. Not that the countryside could be seen, as it was the blackest night that they drove through to get there. The signboard at the gate was the first illuminated object they'd seen since leaving Wadebridge. It read, *Medieval Menus in an Authentick Atmosphere.* 'Oh-oh,' said Toby.

As it turned out the only concessions to period were the absence of forks and the presence of wenches with low-cut dresses who poured spiced plonk from pewter jugs. The food itself was a reassuringly modern choice of chicken or steak with chips. The restaurant was surprisingly full for a Monday night.

Everyone was just reaching the pleasantly full stage when a plump man who was dressed as a cross between Robin Hood and Bonnie Prince Charlie, mounted a podium and announced the cabaret. At the same moment somebody in a suit and tie appeared behind Toby and said, 'You're on.'

'I beg your pardon?' said Toby.

'Cabaret time. You're on.'

'Cabaret time it may be,' said Toby. 'On, I am not.'

'But all of you…'

'We are not.'

'The cabaret,' boomed the man who was dressed as a cross between Bonnie Prince Charlie and Robin Hood, 'is just about to commence.'

'You are joking, I hope,' said Toby to the man in the suit. 'Otherwise, may I introduce our company manager…?'

'What's the problem?' asked Nick, leaning across the table.

'Listen,' said the man in the suit, his voice a shade lower. 'You lot are the cabaret tonight. You haven't forgotten, I suppose?'

'Forgotten?' said Toby. 'It's the first we've heard.'

'Let's get this straight,' said the man in the suit. 'You are the Gulliver's Travels company, aren't you?'

'Sure we are,' said Nick. 'But we're not your cabaret.'

'I beg your pardon,' said the man in the suit, 'but you are.' His voice was now diminished to an urgent whisper, to which everyone was now paying attention. Throughout the restaurant you could have heard a bone drop.

'The cabaret,' repeated the Bonnie Prince hopefully, 'will commence directly.' Nobody paid him any attention. All eyes were focused on the man in the suit and Toby and Nick.

'Look,' said the man in the suit, 'at this.' He produced from his pocket a sheet of Nathan's unmistakeable letterhead on which Nick, leaning over the left shoulder of the suit, and Toby, leaning over the right shoulder, could clearly read the terms of a contract engaging the Gulliver company to perform a cabaret of their own devising this very day, at this particular venue and at this precise time.

'Jesus!' said Toby.

'There you are,' said the man between the shoulders. 'Black and white.'

'Promises made by other people aren't binding,' suggested Nick wishfully.

'Other people aren't here.' The shoulders began to look quite powerful. 'You are.'

'Maybe,' offered Michael, two places away. 'But we're not your cabaret.'

'There's obviously been a mistake,' came the ringing tones of Peter, a little further down the table. Even without a top B flat people listened to Peter.

'Mistake be damned,' said Shoulders, his voice rising. 'Look ye here. I've paid your master five hundred pounds for this. Mark the receipt here.'

'I mark it perfectly well,' said Peter. 'Yet mark I too that we are the victims of great trickery.'

'Trickery, varlet?' said Shoulders. 'What the hell dost

thou mean?'

'Thou knowest,' interrupted Ian, 'full well what he means. Trickery is trickery.'

'Durst thou, knave,' said the Bonnie Prince Charlie man, 'call my comrade-in-arms a trickler?'

'Trickler?' Peter laughed. 'What meanest that?'

'Trickster then,' said Prince Robin in a surly tone, piqued that his vocabulary had let him down.

'Do you but mark how this becomes him?' jeered Toby. 'In that get-up and all. So young and so un-slender.'

Whereupon the man with shoulders intimated in his best Elizabethan English that if no cabaret was forthcoming they would, peradventure, have to stay behind and do the washing up. To this Peter replied that the seas might swallow up the mobled earth ere he'd do any such thing and everyone else nodded their accord. ('Mobled earth is good,' muttered Prince Robin to himself. 'Mobled earth is very good.')

But the man with shoulders advanced toward Peter. 'Oh braggart vile,' he said, 'and damned furious wight!'

Peter stepped back a pace – braggart he'd been called before, but never wight – and fell over a chair. The shoulders fell on top of him, closely followed by their owner and Jim the Giant, thinking that Peter had been physically attacked, waded in with a cry of, 'Cool it, cullions,' which was all he could think of in the heat of the moment. A second later everyone was involved in the scuffle. Prince Robin's cap fell off and two tables were somehow overturned in his efforts to get it back. No-one was hurt, which was fortunate and the goblets and platters, although they had spilled their cargoes widely on the floor, were pretty well undamaged as they were largely made of plastic. On the other hand the noise was tremendous and the mess was approaching the genuinely medieval.

A spontaneous burst of applause rose from the ranks of the non-combatant diners and cheering broke out. Moments later the rafters were actually ringing with echoes of orders for more wine.

By now the minions and scullions from the kitchens had joined the fray, armed with pot-hooks and barding-needles, trivet-clamps and poultry-shears. A preliminary bombardment with bread rolls provoked prompt retaliation and soon the battle escalated as first salvoes of orange peel and then of chicken bones were launched. The audience was enraptured. But then the ammunition began to run out.

It looked to Fran dangerously possible that real kitchen hardware would be deployed, and then who knew where it might end. Judging the moment right to bring the engagement to a close she produced from her bosom the referee's whistle that she always kept there in case of unwelcome approaches from unwanted men in the night-time streets and blew a long loud blast on it. The battle stopped dead.

'Curtain call,' hissed Peter in a professional whisper, and everyone gathered together to take a bow. 'From the centre, from the centre,' Peter had to whisper towards some of the scullions who were threatening to make the line ragged in their eagerness, by bending over too soon.

The audience went wild. When the applause had died down, the chicken bones had been picked up, the bacon-tongs and pastry chisels had been put back in their boxes and the scullions and minions returned to their lairs, everyone present congratulated the actors and management alike on the spectacle. It had been the best cabaret ever staged at the Giant's Castle, they all said. So spontaneously entered upon, so full of life, so loosely scripted, that it might have been a real brawl.

'The art whereby art is concealed,' said the man with suit and shoulders modestly, rearranging some dandruff as he spoke with a deft flick of the hand. Then he ordered fresh goblets of wine and after-dinner mints to set before the Gulliver company while they waited for their taxis to arrive. He told them he very much appreciated their contribution to the evening, that he hoped they would come again and that he would be writing to Nathan to thank him for providing such an excellent service.

'Damn Nathan' said Toby.

'I wonder what he'll dream up next,' said Ian.

'Send us to a research institute?' suggested Philip.

'That's not as remote a possibility as you might

imagine,' said Toby more sombrely than was usual. 'But – ah – here come the goblets of wine and the peppermints. Enjoy them while ye may.'

A Lucky Break

'What happens when Susan stops thinking she's a sea-lion and wants to come back?' Ian asked Nick. 'Nathan seems pretty set on my staying on in the role of Glumdalclitch. Advance bookings have quadrupled…'

'That wasn't hard,' said Nick.

'…And look like going through the roof.' Ian was noticeably less inclined to let himself be interrupted than formerly.

Nick's phone rang before he could reply to this. He picked it up. 'No,' he said. 'Really?' he queried. 'Good God,' he remarked. 'You don't say,' he observed. 'OK,' he finished, 'I'll tell him.' He hung up.

'You're keeping the part,' he said to Ian. 'That's the answer to your question. That was Nathan. There's been some trouble with No Pyjamas. Marian – who's playing Binky, you know – has had a row with the director, walled out of rehearsal and out of the show. It's all most convenient, don't you see? Nathan has offered Binky to Susan, all six foot seven of her, she's jumped at it like a fish… And you get to keep the part of Glumdalclitch, and you go onto a principal's salary as from now, backdated to last Thursday at five minutes to seven.'

'Life seems to be happening very quickly at the moment,' said Ian.

'That's because you're getting older,' said Nick.

Ian spent the next weekend at Collingtree Mansions. Over a lunchtime pint in the Alexandra with Mike Pike he had the opportunity to notice three things. First, that Mike asked him for the loan of a tenner, not just the usual fiver, secondly that Mike was ever so mildly flirting with him (something Mike had never done before) and thirdly, that Mike's normally fresh-looking face which was inclined to be freckly had taken on a greenish tinge. So indeed had his normally candid blue eyes. Ian asked him about this.

'It must be envy,' said Mike matter-of-factly, candour rushing back to his eyes and cheeks. 'You've had a great stroke of luck – I mean talent – and it's only natural that I'm jealous. I mean, it wouldn't be healthy not to be.'

'I suppose it wouldn't be,' said Ian. 'But don't forget that only last month it was you that had the great new job in the West End (which you've still got) and I was just the provincial ASM. In any case, I keep lending you money. You keep paying it back. Nothing really changes. But you'll get your break. Don't worry. It'll happen. You might not even have to sleep with Nathan.'

'Do you really think not?' said Mike, his eyes wide-open with relief. 'I wish I could be so sure. Marian wouldn't have got where she did otherwise and neither, I hear, would Susan. ...Who is coming into rehearsal tomorrow by the way. It'll be interesting to have an eight-foot Binky. All the men will get cricks in their necks, except yours truly, face-down on the floor.'

Ian had to leave after lunch The next Gulliver date was to be at Coatbridge in Scotland, which would take quite a while to get to, even on a Lion room budget. The week after that, while Nathan banked the proceeds of the ninety-two percent attendance there, Gulliver went to Cowbridge in South Wales, then north again to Llanfairpwllgwyngyllgogerychwyrndrobwllllantysiliogo gogoch on Anglesey, so that Ian did not return to Collingtree Mansions for several weeks.

Mike Pike was there – at Collingtree Mansions, that is,   not   at Llanfairpwllgwyngyllgogerychwyrndrobwllllantysiliogo gogoch – on one of those intervening Sunday mornings, sitting with Marta in her kitchen and eating thick slices of wholemeal toast that dripped with hot butter and honey. Marta was not obliged to provide breakfast for her tenants but from goodness of heart and in the tradition of the vanished Irish aristocracy from which her forbears had come, she usually did. Especially if the tenants were young, poor, artistic and thinner than the national average. Which they usually were.

'Couldn't you have said no?' Marta was asking. 'Surely you could have said no.' For Mike had just catalogued the extra demands his company manager had been making of him during the previous two weeks, the try-out of Yes We Have No Pyjamas. Revolving the revolving flat, for example, doing the off-stage door-slam at the end of the first scene, checking the props table at the start of Act One when he should have been getting into character as the corpse…

'In theory, yes,' said Mike. 'I suppose I could have said no. They're jobs for the stage crew, not for an acting ASM stroke understudy. But the crew's been a bit stretched with Doreen off sick and they're not going to get an extra casual in just to slam a door… Besides, for every young actor who won't muscle in and help a bit there's twenty on the dole queue who will. No, I shouldn't grumble really. It's all part of being a dogsbody which, let's face it, is what I am.'

'What you need,' said Marta, as she had said a hundred times before to Mike and the many like him who had found sanctuary at 9c Collingtree Mansions, 'what you need is a lucky break.'

The door opened and Paul put his head round it. He wanted to know if the music room was available.

'Yes, Paul,' said Marta, surprised to see him on a Sunday. He explained that he had an extra lesson the next morning and needed to polish up the Appassionata. Marta offered him toast and coffee but he declined politely, saying he had better go and get started.

'He works so hard, so hard,' said Marta when Paul had left the room, and she shook her head, heavy with the wisdom of the years, as if to say that that was never enough. She poured more coffee for herself and Mike. 'Mrs Mahooda flooded the kitchen again yesterday,' she said conversationally. 'She doesn't seem to have the hang of the washing-machine. If only she'd put the waste-pipe in the bath like everybody else. I went upstairs as soon as it started to come through, but her English is so poor that by the time I'd made her understand the damage was done. Then she presented me with a huge sponge cake. I could hardly complain after that.'

Mike Pike went out to get the papers. Stepping out of the faded Edwardian elegance of Marta's flat, where the air was now thunderous with Beethoven, he abruptly entered the seedier world of the communal stairs. Mrs Timothy was obviously still keeping busy in 9e: one of her satisfied customers was climbing furtively downstairs as Mike came out onto the landing. The Mahoodas in 9d were obviously out to judge from the silence, and the Italians in 9b were obviously in, to judge from the noise. Miss Toil who lived down in 9a had her blinds down so she was presumably still in bed or simply dead. Mike walked out into the spring sunshine while the sound of Marta's glorious Bechstein, moulded under Paul's fleet fingers, floated like bells overhead.

In the middle of the afternoon the flat was empty save for Mike (if you didn't count the bed-ridden Max). Marta had gone out with her niece, Paul had returned to his Earls Court basement, while the only other person who might have been there, Alice, was away for the weekend. Mike made his way to the music room, taking advantage of the flat's emptiness to try over a new song he was learning as a possible future audition piece. He was not a bad singer, though by no means a good one, and the same went for his efforts at the keyboard. However his attempts to both play and sing at the same time were great trials to him and he took care always to conduct them in camera. He was just halfway through a brave but halting rendering of *Something's Coming* from West Side Story when the door shot violently open and a bright blue face peered round it. 'Jesus Christ!' Mike said. 'Alice, is that you? You nearly gave me a heart attack.'

'I'm sorry Mike,' said the blue face.

'I thought you were away,' mumbled Mike, sounding a little sheepish. 'I thought the flat was empty – except for Max. Why is your face that extraordinary colour?' A thought struck him and he peered closely at the floor-length dressing-gown Alice was wearing. 'You're not that colour all over, are you?'

'No,' said Alice. 'Just the face. It's a new beauty pack I'm trying. I came back early. I've got an audition tomorrow. That's why… I mean, I heard you in here and wondered if you'd mind going through a song for me.' She pulled a rolled-up sheet of music from one of her dressing-gown sleeves and waved it at him. 'I haven't sung in ages. What were you practising when I came in?'

'Something's Coming,' said Mike.

'But not the Something's Coming from West Side Story...'

'Well ... er ... yes,' said Mike, sounding a little pained. 'What's your audition for anyway?'

'Just a little fringe thing in Finchley,' said Alice. 'But beggars can't be choosers. I've been stuck in the mud at the bottom of the typing pool all winter. At least you're opening in the West End next week.'

I know,' said Mike. 'I should be grateful. But playing a corpse is pretty deadly. I haven't played a live human being on stage since I left drama school.'

'What you need,' said Alice, 'is for your leading man to fall ill. Like Ian's leading lady did. That'd give you a chance at least.'

'Unfortunately Malcolm has the constitution of an ox. There isn't a chance in a million.'

'Then he must fall under a bus or break a leg or something.'

'Well, I wouldn't wish that on him... All the same, a little painless laryngitis for a few days would do no harm.'

'What is the exact date of your West End press night?' Alice asked. To Mike's astonishment she pulled a pencil and a shorthand pad out of her dressing-gown pocket.

'Wednesday week,' said Mike.

'Right.' Alice made a note. 'So that's the date everyone's working to. And that is the night you have to be on instead of Malcolm.'

'Well, in an ideal situa...'

'Listen, Mike. This is what you have to do. First you must buy a lemon.'

'A lemon?'

'Yes. A lemon. The next time there's a moon – its best if there's a full one but it's not essential – you cut the lemon in quarters by the moon's light ... along the middle rib, mind ... and you put one quarter under each leg of your bed.'

'You what?!' Mike exploded with laughter.

'I'm serious. One of our gardeners out in Kenya told me this. Just listen. You open the window, get into bed, then you think very positively, very positively indeed, about the illness or accident you want Malcolm to have...' Alice couldn't go on. Mike had collapsed over the piano keyboard, shaking with laughter, and Alice had caught the giggles from him. 'I'm serious,' she kept trying to say, but in the end she had to give up.

'Come on.' Mike pulled himself together at last. 'Let's have a look at this song of yours. Alice handed him her sheet music. 'Oh no,' he said, his brow furrowing. 'Five sharps!'

The day of the London press night of Yes We Have No Pyjamas began badly. Mike had been up late the previous night rehearsing, and there was to be a final dress run this afternoon before the evening performance at seven thirty. Emerging from his room at Collingtree Mansions at mid-day he found Paul munching a slice of cake in the hall while Marta's kitchen swam with water. 'It's Mrs Mahooda again,' explained Marta, mop in hand.

'Oh dear,' said Mike. 'She's such a nice person otherwise.

'I don't expect they have much water in Morocco,' said Paul innocently. 'These cakes she sends down are splendid, though.'

'She saw the Queen on Thursday,' said Marta. 'When she was on Walkabout in the City. She queued all day. She passed right by her and she smiled and then she waved a Union Jack.'

'Heavens,' said Mike, his imagination struggling to get the picture right. 'The Queen waved a Union Jack?'

'No,' said Marta. 'Mrs Mahooda did.'

'No less remarkable,' said Mike. 'Now I must go. Dress rehearsal.'

'Have a nice day,' said Paul through cake.

On the stairs Mike met Mrs Mahooda in person. 'I hear you saw the Queen the other day,' he said.

Mrs Mahooda looked at him with big compassionate eyes. 'I know. I sorry. I leave the tap running.'

Mike had expected to find a certain amount of tension in the air at the theatre. Adrenalin was his profession's life blood. But he hadn't expected the atmosphere of total panic that assailed him at the stage door. 'Where've you been? Where the hell have you been?' The company manager's staring eyes seemed ready to roll down his cheeks. 'I've been ringing your number for an hour. I keep getting a prostitute.'

'That's Mrs Timothy upstairs,' explained Mike.

'Malcolm's not here,' went on the company manager. 'They rang from the hospital. He's still in casualty. They don't even know if he'll make the show. Nathan's coming over at three o'clock. They'll decide then whether the press night is cancelled. Meanwhile the dress is to go ahead. You've got to read in for Malcolm.'

'No,' said Mike with a coolness which surprised even himself and left the company manager for once speechless. 'I will not be reading in for Malcolm. I will not be reading Malcolm's part. I know every word of it. Though you may not remember, that is what I was originally contracted to do. Now I'd better get along to wardrobe, hadn't I, and sort out the costume. By the way, what did happen to Malcolm?'

'He fell out of a window watering his window-boxes. They think he's cracked some ribs.'

'Goodness me,' said Mike absently. His mind was already racing far ahead: he was planning the details of his eye make-up.

Malcolm didn't do the show that night. The management didn't cancel. Mike Pike went on. The buzz afterwards was tremendous. 'Darling, darling, darling Mike,' said the company manager. 'You were wonderful, wonderful, wonderful.'

The whole company went on to a club afterwards. By the time they left the early editions of the morning papers were already out. They were all very complimentary about Susan's performance as Binky ... which was just as well actually ... because they were ecstatic about Mike Pike's...

'The sheer energy of this young actor breathed un-looked-for life into this paunchy middle-aged comedy,' wrote Hilton Ullman. 'Michael Pike is among the bravest new talent of the decade,' wrote Mervyn Cawdle. While Leonard Bevin managed to accord him six consecutive clauses of praise, each with its own semi-colon, between one full-stop and the next.

Mike Pike walked all the way home, though walking hardly came into it. He ran, he skipped, he sang *Something's Coming* at the top of his voice, he thrashed his way through the fencing sequence he had learnt for a drama-school production of Romeo and Juliet and never forgotten; the moon shone brightly on him and he felt as though he was flying.

With a little effort he managed to find Collingtree Mansions and turn his latch-key in the door. Then he crept upstairs and let himself into number C. The hallway was in darkness but to his surprise there was a light – and voices – coming from his own room. He flung open the door. There sat Alice, and Marta, and Paul. Through a haze of cigarette smoke he could see Mrs Mahooda, and Mrs Timothy with a client, sitting demurely on his bed. They were all drinking champagne.

'Here's a glass for you, Mike,' said Marta, beaming as she poured it out.

'Well done, mate' said Paul. 'You're all over the papers.'

'Sit down, Mike,' said Alice. 'You look gob-smacked. Now do tell me. Did you do what I told you to – with the moon and the lemon quarters?'

'No,' said Mike. 'Good heavens, no. Of course not!'

'Well, never mind,' said Marta with a beatific mile. 'We all did.'

Board Games

'That's the most extraordinary thing I ever heard,' Ian said to Mike Pike the next weekend over their Sunday morning pint in The Alexandra. 'But I'm ever so happy for you. I read all the reviews. All the same I can't believe that thing about the lemons.'

'Have I ever lied to you before?' asked Mike.

Ian shrugged his shoulders. 'Only you can know the answer to that.'

'It's a funny thing,' said Mike thoughtfully.

'What is?' asked Ian.

'What people believe. Generally speaking they believe what isn't true quite easily. But it's different when you try to tell them the truth.'

'I see,' said Ian. 'I don't think I'd ever thought of that.'

'Anyway,' said Mike. 'You don't have to take my word for it. Check with Marta if you like. Ask Paul. Mrs Mahooda. Mrs Timothy…'

'OK,' conceded Ian. 'I'll believe you. Anyway, lucky you.'

'Lucky you too,' Mike reminded Ian. 'Still playing Glumdalclitch… Where to tomorrow?'

'Nathan's found another town that ends with …bridge,' Ian told him. 'This one's called Robertsbridge. The Bland Memorial Theatre. In darkest Sussex.'

One day later, by which time Mike had taken the bus to his new place of work in the West End, Ian and the whole Gulliver company had found their way to Robertsbridge. Word had arrived here already that the show was not to be missed and the advance bookings stood at eighty-nine percent by teatime. By seven o'clock there was a queue round the block for returned tickets – a queue that the members of the board of directors of the Bland Memorial Theatre could not help noticing as they filed in, by a side door, to the theatre's principal office and boardroom, which were one and the same room. But they viewed the queue that snaked around the building not with feelings of pride and jubilation but of exasperation and bitterness. For they were arriving to attend a meeting whose agenda read as follows:

1. Minutes of the Last Meeting.

2. Matters Arising.

3. Accountant's Report.

4. Arrangements for Final Closure of the Bland Memorial Theatre and Winding Up of Bland Memorial Theatre Company Ltd.

5. Any Other Business.

Conversation was suitably subdued as the board members greeted one another. In marked contrast the roar of an excited audience echoed down the corridors and rattled at the door. There came a smart rap on the table.

'Ladies and gentlemen, I declare the meeting open. I'd like, if possible, to keep this sad occasion short.' Councillor Leviticus Bland had opened the meeting. 'I'm sure you'd all agree.'

'Yes,' and, 'Hear, hear,' agreed the other members.

'Item one. Min…'

'Propose the minutes be taken as…'

'Seconded…'

'Item two. Matters arising from the minutes.'

The accountant shuffled his papers, awaiting the surely imminent moment when he would have to get to his feet. The chairman's boot-button eyes darted, focusing and refocusing, defying anyone to thwart the onward momentum of the meeting.

'One moment, Mr Chairman…' This was Sir Plunkett Bland. Momentum crunched to a halt.

'Yes, Sir Plunkett?' crackled the chairman.

'According to the minutes,' said Sir Plunkett, now standing and waving his sheaf of papers, 'I'm supposed to have heartily agreed with the proposal set out in item two, annexe four. In point of fact I said I heartily disagreed.'

'Yes, yes,' said the chairman. His hands appeared to be brushing crumbs from the table and his twin gimlet eyes were abruptly turned on the company secretary. 'Dracula, will you see to it?'

'Yes,' said Dracula, removing a cigarette from between his thin lips and dipping his secretarial quill into the ink-well. There was a scratch and a splash and the accountant was obliged to wipe his eye with a forefinger. 'It's done,' said Dracula.

'And shall you correct the copies as well?' enquired the chairman coolly.

'Directly after the meeting,' said Dracula with a tiny little bow of the head.

'Now perhaps…' continued the chairman.

'I'm sorry,' said Councillor Sixtus Bland, getting to his feet, 'but I can't accept the minutes' interpretation of our collective reaction to the production of Jaws that we hosted in February. It may indeed have been a box-office near-success. Yet I feel I must place on record my revulsion at the subject matter. It was not at all the same story as we'd been led to expect from seeing the film. This kind of backstairs view of life in a brothel may be good for the box office, but frankly I was appalled.'

Everyone in the room silently wrote the number six on their blotter. This was in accordance with the rules of a game that had been played at the Bland Memorial Theatre since time immemorial to enliven dull board meetings. There were five points to be scored each time Sixtus said he was appalled, plus one extra point each time he said *frankly*.

'What's more,' Sixtus added, 'my wife…'

Everyone wrote the figure two.

'…was appalled' (That made another seven points. If he were now to mention his daughter…)

'And my daughter saw the show twice. She was appalled twice. I was appalled that she was appalled. And frankly my wife…'

'Have you got a calculator?' Dracula hissed to the accountant.

'Shh!' said the accountant. 'I'm counting. I'll circulate the score afterwards.'

'…My wife was appalled.'

The chairman wrote the figure twenty on his blotter. Then, 'Would you make a note of Mr Bland's views?' he said to Dracula. 'Thank you, Mr Bland. Any other matters arising?'

'Yes, Mr Chairman,' said Councillor Mrs Marjorie Bland, taking the floor. 'The income from the book-stall is minuted as being two pounds and eleven pence for the month of February. However my daughter – who, as you know, works on the book-stall – has stated quite clearly that she sold a copy of War and Peace during that month, as well as one of the Hilary Clinton biography. Now that must surely come to more than two pounds and eleven.'

'Perhaps the accountant can account for it,' said the chairman, swivelling his head in that officer's direction like a tank turret.

'Of course,' said the accountant. 'The profitable months are evened out against the unprofitable ones by a process that we accountants call accrual. Month by month the figures may not be exact but at the end of the year they should be correct to the penny, I think you'll find.'

Everybody wrote the figure four. That was the score to be notched up whenever the accountant said, 'I think you'll find'.

'Why is this accruing necessary with such small sums?' asked Councillor Stuart Bland.

'Because it is impossible to record a zero figure in the accounts,' said the accountant.

'According to what principle of accounting?' asked the chairman, genuinely astonished.

'Because,' said the hapless accountant, 'the nought on the computer keyboard is broken. So is the dash. There hasn't been any money in the budget for a new one for three years. I've kept asking.'

'Do you mean,' said Sir Plunkett Bland, 'that all the figures submitted to the board over the last three years have been erroneous due to a broken keyboard?'

'I think you'll find that that is the case,' said the accountant.

'I'm appalled,' said Sixtus Bland. 'Frankly I'm appalled.'

(Eleven points. Right?)

'Perhaps this would be an appropriate moment,' said the chairman in a voice of tungsten, 'to move on to item three: the accountant's report.'

'Just one more point...' This was Jeremy Bland, the youngest member of the board, now rising elegantly from his chair. He was smoking through a long ebony cigarette holder.

'Yes?' bit the chairman, as if on a bullet.

Jeremy drew languidly on his cigarette before replying. 'My dears...'

Everyone jotted down three. That was the score every time Jeremy addressed the board as my dears.

'My dears, I feel it is too, too dreadful to limit the report of the annual drag contest to a mere one line and a half. Those measly minutes. To think that my own appearance – for the last time, it now appears – on the Robertsbridge boards should be recorded only in the phrase *including Jeremy Bland* is too awfully distressing. Could not some mention have been made of the Chanel suit, the Yves St-Laurent scarf and the custom-tailored corsets? Nor even the Pirelli shoes and the Amora lipstick? Surely you must appreciate the importance of recording these small refinements, especially in the last delicate burp of this ill-fated but nevertheless delightful journal.'

'This is too much,' interploded Sir Plunkett Bland. 'I don't know why we've put up with this prehistoric pansy on the board for the last five years in the first place. That we should have to bow out of existence with a panegyric to his degraded tastes is altogether out of the question.'

'I can't help agreeing with you – through the chair – said Sixtus Bland. 'While being more enlightened than Sir Plunkett I must say that I too am appalled by Jeremy's lack of seriousness. As no doubt we all are. We must all be appalled. We must, of course, accept the presence of the homosexual lifestyle as part of the warp and woof of the theatre, even, dare I say it, here at Robertsbridge in the darkest depths of Sussex, but do we, frankly, can we, must we, accept having the beastly thing rammed down our throats?'

'Am I to minute this?' Dracula asked the chairman.

For reply the chairman just looked at Dracula and Dracula had the impression of being scrutinised by a Garibaldi biscuit, a face divided into two identical rectangles, offering an approximately flat if shiny surface, from which a pair of eyes stared unwinkingly, like two very small currants.

'Item three,' announced the chairman in a voice that defied further interruption. 'The accountant's report.'

'Mr Chairman...' began the accountant.

'Objection, Mr Bland,' said Mr Bland. 'How can he make a report at all when his computer can't produce an accurate figure?'

'With respect,' said the chairman, 'he merely said that it didn't write noughts.'

'And whoever saw a balance sheet without noughts on it?' asked Sir Plunkett Bland.

'You all did,' replied the accountant. 'For three years. Nobody objected.'

'Outrageous!' squeaked Jeremy Bland.

'Order,' said Councillor Leviticus Bland. 'Perhaps we can proceed to the more pressing business of item four.'

'Point of procedure,' put in Councillor Stuart Bland. 'Does any one of us know how to close down a theatre or wind up the affairs of a limited company?'

There was a long silence, during which the sound of a happy audience in the distance ate its way into the room like acid. 'Well?' challenged Councillor Stuart Bland. 'Do we?'

Nobody did. Neither Dracula nor the accountant. Nor Sir Plunkett Bland, nor Councillor Leviticus Bland the chairman, nor Mrs Marjorie Bland, nor Sixtus Bland, nor

Jeremy Bland, nor even Lucy Bland, Michael Bland and Richard Bland, who had not spoken during the course of the meeting and never had spoken at any meeting, according to the minutes, since their accession to the board.

So with unanimous approval – a phrase which now made its first and only appearance in the minutes of the meetings of the Bland Memorial Theatre Company Ltd. – the remaining items of the agenda were adjourned for three days, until Thursday.

A Man of Leisure

Following the Board Meeting of the Bland Memorial Theatre, jewel in the cultural crown of Robertsbridge in deepest Sussex, at which the latest disastrous set of financial accounts had put the writing on the wall in the boldest of capital letters, the borough's Director of Recreation, Arts, Culture and Unusual Leisure Activities (Dracula for short) had been charged by the Board's Chairman, Councillor Leviticus Bland, with making arrangement for the official winding up of the company. But there were other calls on Dracula's time…

At seven-thirty next morning the Director of Recreation, Arts, Culture and Unusual Leisure Activities hauled himself into his office. He looked like death. He felt like death. He felt like a cigarette. He lit his tenth one of the day.

The phone rang. It was the Borough Engineer, about the cracks at the bottom of the swimming pool. He'd come up with a new kind of glue that would do the job quite nicely and harden under water so that it wouldn't be necessary to drain the pool. The glue wasn't actually toxic, provided nobody drank the water. How many people, in Dracula's opinion, actually did?

Dracula said that he hadn't got the exact figure to hand but that he would look it up in the Annual Abstract of Statistics and get back. 'I wish I were dead,' he said to himself as he put the phone down. He was the chairman of the swimming pool committee.

The phone rang again. It was the chairwoman of the poetry society, trying to find a rhyme for sugar. 'Bugger,' said Dracula (he had come from the North originally) and hung up. He was the treasurer of the poetry society. He lit another cigarette. It took him one minute and seventeen seconds to smoke a cigarette in theory, though in practice he was interrupted more often than not by the telephone. When he wasn't, he compensated by smoking the filter tip as well. Why not? At least it only tasted disgusting. It didn't do you any harm – as far as anyone could tell.

His secretary arrived at nine. 'Thank God you're here,' said Dracula. 'I'm dying.'

'I know,' said Sonia. 'So is the geranium. You haven't watered it again.'

'It's not my job to water the plants, Sonia. It's the only thing I'm able to delegate with a clear conscience. Why, oh why don't the plants get watered?'

'Because you're very bad at delegating. You say so yourself. Now I'm going to make myself some coffee. Would you like one?'

'Yes please, but do be quick. There's no end of stuff to get through. The Bland Memorial Theatre's closing down and I've got to find out how one goes about winding the place up. I don't suppose you'd know, by any chance?'

'No,' said Sonia. 'I've never closed a theatre.'

'No,' said Dracula, 'I don't suppose you have.'

Sonia was gone a half-hour. During this time
Dracula answered the phone, first to the refuse
collectors who'd had an altercation with the staff of
the Baltic Blues Bar about a completely comatose
customer they had found in one of the dustbins,
secondly to the manager of the Goldfish Cinema who
was complaining of a strange smell in the gentlemen's
lavatory. ('Open the window,' was Dracula's advice.
'There isn't one.' was the reply. Dracula offered the
extension number of the Borough Engineer.) Thirdly
to the Borough Engineer again. Who said, 'How dare
you give my extension number away like this! One
more time and I'm volunteering yours to the Inland
Revenue, the Encyclopaedia Britannica and the
Spanish Inquisition.'

Then, just as Sonia walked in through the door,
coffee cup in hand, the chairman of the Bland
Memorial Theatre phoned and talked for an hour and
thirty-five minutes.

After which time, 'I expect my coffee's cold by
now,' Dracula said to Sonia who was reading the
newspaper.

'Not at all,' said Sonia. 'I forgot to make it. Look,

why don't you go and make us both a cup? I can look after the phone for a minute.'

Dracula lit a cigarette. 'Listen Sonia. I must – I really have to – take a break. I haven't had a holiday since nineteen-eighty nine. I've had two children since then and I haven't had time to ask them their names. I think one of them's a boy and the other's a girl but it's difficult to tell when I only ever see them in bed asleep. My wife knows for sure but I haven't had a chance to ask her. And so I'm taking tomorrow off.'

'Taking tomorrow off?' Sonia's eyes widened in disbelief. 'With the Druids' Eisteddfod on Wednesday?'

'Damn the Druids.'

'And the Bland board meeting on Thursday.'

'Bugger the Blands.'

'The hanging-basket society meeting is tomorrow.'

'Hang the hanging-baskets.'

Sonia bit her lip. She had been about to mention the Fabian Freemasons' function the following Friday but thought better of it.

At that moment the geranium collapsed with an audible flop and Sonia, overcome by a rare compassion, rushed to the kitchen where she administered iced water and left it to recover lying on its side in the vegetable compartment of the fridge.

While Sonia was out of the room Dracula answered the phone to the Borough Chimney-Sweep who had been sent to the Goldfish Cinema by the Borough Engineer. ('Where is the chimney?' he wanted to know.

'There isn't one,' Dracula answered.

'What am I supposed to do then?'

'Just find something to sweep and sweep it.')

Sixtus Bland also telephoned to check that his name would be spelt correctly in the amended minutes for the last but one Bland board meeting. Then Jeremy Bland rang for the same reason and immediately afterwards the Brown Toilet-paper Lady rang to see if the Recreation, Arts, Culture and Unusual Leisure Activities department wanted to buy an especially large quantity of brown toilet-paper at an especially reasonable price. 'Normally my secretary deals with the paperwork,' said Dracula. 'Unfortunately she's with the geranium just at present. Let me give you the extension number of the Borough Engineer.'

Five minutes later there was a phone call from the Inland Revenue and immediately Dracula had disentangled himself from the coils of that conversation there came a tap at the door from a bright-eyed young man with a hire-purchase agreement in his hand and an encyclopaedia in the car-park.

It was three o'clock by the time Dracula had dealt with these two demands on his time and nearly five o'clock before he had got rid of the shy but persuasive young man in a red-buttoned cassock who announced himself as the Apostolic

Under-Secretary of Information. He had with him an immensely long questionnaire which began, 'Who made you?' and ended, 'What are the Four Last Things?' Dracula had some trouble with the second question, though he felt sure that at least one of them would be a cigarette.

During this time Dracula watched Sonia eat two sandwiches, drink seven more cups of coffee, skim the Guardian and devour the Sun. Now she was looking at her watch.

'Sonia,' Dracula said when the Apostolic Visitor had left with his findings, 'I will not be here tomorrow. Is that clear? Would you bear that in mind? And will you get the geranium out of the fridge right away? Whether it lives or whether it dies, the deciding moment is surely past by now.'

Sonia turned and went without a word, then reappeared with the geranium, upright but looking a little bewildered, on top of a huge pile of documents, files, faxes, reports and memoranda. 'Seeing as how you won't be in tomorrow, perhaps you ought to go through this little lot before you go home. Clear the decks, you know. Anyway, I don't expect you'll be needing me any more this evening so I'll be off.'

The phone rang soon after Sonia left. Dracula let it ring. He lit a cigarette. He read the annual report of the schoolteachers' leisure committee, corrected their spelling and added his comments before retyping it. He left a message on his wife's answer-phone to say that he would be home late and went out for more cigarettes.

The cash-flow projection for the philatelic society occupied him till nearly midnight and the bilingual writing up of the minutes of the Esperanto Institute took him until half-past three. He was still working on the planning application to increase the depth of ice on the skating-rink by nought point six centimetres when Sonia arrived to begin work the next morning. As she disappeared to make coffee the telephone rang. It was the chairman of the Bland theatre. 'Have you got everything sorted yet?' Councillor Leviticus Bland wanted to know.

'Well no, not exactly.'

'Good Lord, you've had all day and all night!'

'I do have other responsibilities you know.'

'Maybe, maybe. But this must be sorted out. Otherwise what can we say to the board on Thursday? How can we conduct the meeting? You and I must get together this evening. Eight o'clock? Good. Can you have all the papers ready? With all the information from our solicitors, the bank, the auditors and Companies House? Or at all events make sure there's lots of paper. Documents with clauses and sub-clauses, annexes and attachments. It makes everyone feel so much … safer. I'm afraid it may turn into an all-nighter. Are there any papers you think I should bring?'

'Yes,' said Dracula with only the smallest pause for thought. 'Green Rizlas – and a couple of ounces of flake.'

Jumble

'But who is Bland?' asked Toby after Tuesday's show.

'They're all Bland,' said Nick.

'But who is the Bland Memorial Theatre a memorial to?'

'No-one can remember,' said Nick. 'When everybody in the town has the same surname it's very difficult to know which individual is being honoured at any given moment. At the same time, of course, it means that every family in the town can bask in the same glory.'

'Like being British.'

'Exactly.'

'Then long live the Blands,' said Toby. 'But seriously, why are they closing?'

'Money,' said Nick.

'Ask a silly question,' I suppose, said Toby. 'You might have answered "scandal" and we'd have been fascinated, probed for details and so on. You might have said "terms of the will". Nice little story for the cuttings book. You might have said "death-watch in the roof" or even "death-wish" or "terminal decadence" and all the ologists and osophers and osophists could have had a field day – as well as us, of course. But you say the word money and the conversation is at an end. We are transported in an instant into the real world. How unspeakably depressing. We bury ourselves in culture up to the neck, we travel the country bruisingly in its name – even when the execution falls somewhat short of the ideal, as now – and yet we still trip over this monumental, idiotic stumbling-block of a word – money.

'I hate to be picky,' said Michael, 'but I don't think money is the problem. It's the lack of it.'

Toby glared at him.

'Sorry,' said Michael as quietly as he could.

'But how come it's closing?' asked Ian. 'We're playing to packed houses.'

'Yes, but it's the first time in years,' said Nick. 'They're technically bankrupt. Local government's bailed them out over the years. Now they've got to stop.'

'So when does it close?' Ian asked.

'Saturday night. As soon as our sets are on the lorry the dock doors'll be closed for the last time. And when the last member of the audience walks up the aisle the chandelier will go out for ever, leaving the gilded cherubs to end their days in darkness. Though I suppose the office staff will have to come in on Monday to clear their desks on the way to the dole office.'

'That's terrible,' said Ian, who was visibly upset.

'And ours will be the show that closed the theatre.'

'Technically speaking, yes,' said Toby. 'That's how it'll read in the history books.'

'But what a reflection on us,' said Ian. 'We must do something. Stop it happening.'

'What do you suggest?' said Michael. 'Pay off their overdraft? Lie down in the path of the man from the electricity board?'

'Steady on,' said Toby.

'Because seriously, nothing less than that is even going to dent the problem. And unless…'

'We could do a benefit performance on Sunday,' said Ian brightly. You know, announce it every night, put ads in the paper. People'd come.'

'You'd get three thousand ponds at most. Oh, maybe six thousand if you were really cheeky with the ticket prices. It's still only a drop in the ocean. And five days isn't very long to publicise it in.'

'We could have a jumble sale.'

'You're joking!' said Michael. 'Hours of work for everyone and you end up with a hundred pounds and a few unsaleable odd socks for wardrobe spares.'

'That wasn't quite the sort of jumble sale I had in mind,' said Ian. 'First thing tomorrow I'm going to see the management. Now I'm off to bed.'

'Frankly I worry about him,' said Toby. 'Being a cross-dressing star seems to be changing him. And not in quite the way I might have hoped.'

'It's not a change in him at all,' said Michael. 'Remember Holly Bush, and how he sorted her out? Getting rid of those thieving kids…'

'Ah yes,' said Toby. 'I wonder how that went…'

The next morning Ian was closeted in the theatre office from nine until ten thirty, at which time he disappeared into the town. At eleven thirty he was spotted struggling back with a very heavily laden wheelbarrow containing a bland-new computer, complete with all the bits including a keyboard that would do noughts and dashes. (The man in the shop had assured him of this.) Ian had negotiated for the theatre to have the equipment on indefinite loan (he hadn't been as ASM for nothing) in return for a subliminal mention of the supplier's name (Bland) on the theatre's public address system twice nightly for the foreseeable future. At mid-day Ian asked Nick if he could call a special meeting of the Gulliver company during the afternoon. 'Nathan knows all about it,' he said breezily.

Remarkably, almost everyone turned up. Ian took the chair with an air of confidence that was nevertheless so unassuming that nobody questioned it. 'I have a proposal to put to you. It concerns the future of this theatre. If you are in favour of what I have to suggest we shall put it to the theatre board and then to the owners of the building – that's the Borough Council. In practice exactly the same individuals make up both bodies but they like to be approached twice, with different hats on, for the sake of form.'

'We have to wear different hats when we go to see them?' checked Philip.

'No,' said Nick. 'They do. And they're not real hats.'

'Well, I don't see…' muttered Philip.

'What I really want to ask you all,' Ian went on, 'is whether you'd all be willing to give up your Sunday to do a benefit performance.'

'I thought that was coming,' said everyone in an aside to the person next to them.

'I don't like to seem selfish,' said Peter, 'but is it unreasonable to ask what we might be getting out of this ourselves?'

'Perfectly reasonable,' said Ian. 'You are assured of the continuing existence of one more showcase for your talent and a beautiful acoustic setting – you've said so yourself – for your top B flat. That applies to us all as individuals. Collectively we shall be remembered in the name of the theatre which, if all goes according to plan, will be renamed The Gulliver Theatre.'

'Good God,' said someone.

'Which brings me to the next point,' said Ian. 'I need

your help in organising a jumble sale.'

'Not the jumble sale!' said Michael. 'I thought we told you…'

'It won't be an ordinary jumble sale,' said Ian. 'This time the theatre is the jumble. The purchasers are the people of Robertsbridge and Nathan in equal proportion.'

'Nathan?!' Exclamation marks ricocheted around the room.

'Listen, it works like this…' and Ian went into the details of his plan. 'So in the end the Council uses the money raised to pay off the theatre's debts (which it was going to have to do anyway) and Nathan and the townspeople start off with a beautiful building and a clean financial slate.'

'Yes, but Nathan?!' Toby still objected. 'Wouldn't it be better for the people to have a car-park on the site, or even a supermarket, than a theatre that was part-owned by Nathan of all people? The man has no soul, no artistic integrity. He's not remotely educated theatrically.'

'There are two possible answers to that,' said Ian, un-fazed. 'The first is that artistic integrity can be acquired as part of the learning process that goes to make up the Whole Man. As for a soul, you can't give a man a soul but (to adapt Aristotle) you can make him behave as if he has one. And the contract that Nathan would be bound to – that is, to consult the wishes of the theatre patrons, his partners along with ourselves in this venture, would ensure that he behaved just so. That is the first answer.'

There was a thunderous silence. Nobody had ever heard Ian string an argument together, let alone quote Aristotle in his support.

'Alternatively,' Ian continued, 'if Nathan doesn't change his spots it'll be because the people of Robertsbridge deserve him as he is, unregenerate and unrepentant. In which case no harm is done, the customers are satisfied and there will still be a Gulliver Theatre where Peter's top notes can ring out to perfection and where Toby will be happy to come and direct a play for Nathan at the first mention of a fee. Right, Toby?'

'I suppose you're right,' Toby agreed reluctantly. 'But what about this binding commitment to consult the wishes of the Robertsbridgers? How is that going to work? Are you going to draft it?'

'No, of course not,' said Ian. 'But according to the theatre manager here they've got this tame man who works for the Council, is secretary to the board, and who can do anything with pieces of paper. He's called Dracula and he can tie people up in contracts that even Houdini couldn't get out of.'

'Impressive,' said Nick. 'He's certainly going to need all his skills to tie up Nathan. But with a name like Dracula I suppose he's off to a good start.'

'Thank you,' said Ian. 'So can we have a show of

hands, pleas? Those in favour of the whole package…?'

And so it came about that, after Ian had phoned Nathan, Nathan had phoned Councillor Leviticus Bland, and the last had phoned Dracula, the process of closing down the theatre was thrown into reverse gear and the papers that the chairman and Dracula worked on throughout Wednesday night – with the exceptions of the ones that Dracula rolled up, filled with tobacco and smoked – were concerned with the sale of the building in several thousand tiny lots, each with its own parcel of rights, privileges and responsibilities. Finally the contract that would bind Nathan inextricably into this web was drafted by Dracula – on the unofficial advice of the Guliver company – on fly-paper.

It was already seven o'clock on Thursday morning by the time the paper spells were woven. 'You look all-in,' said the chairman to Dracula. 'You should take the day off between now and the meeting.'

'Could you possibly make that an order?' asked Dracula.

That night Ian made an impassioned curtain-speech after the performance in which, in confident and capable tones, he invited the audience to stake a claim to any piece of the theatre they took a fancy to and could afford. They were able to do this by attaching signed cheques to bits of the building and its equipment. Usherettes stood ready with ice-cream trays around their necks that were full of rolls of Selotape, 'to make sure,' as Ian put it, 'that the promises stick.'

Then the audience was led by the actors, the stage crew and the theatre staff, to each and every corner of the building. Antlike they threaded their way up the ladders and along the catwalks of the fly tower. The hardiest climbed up to the pulley-grid and the smoke vents and some even scaled the queasy paint-frame. Others burrowed in procession beneath the stage, to the furniture store, to the boiler room, into the warm opulent darkness of the curtain store, where – the story was later told – a number of close friendships were struck up between people who had never met before. Everywhere cheques blossomed, fluttering in the draughts on their Selotape stalks. It went on till well past midnight.

On Saturday the drill was repeated, both at the matinee and the evening performance. By the early hours of Sunday morning there was hardly a brick or a radiator that hadn't been claimed in perpetuity by someone. After the Sunday benefit performance it was found necessary to lead the audience out onto the roof under floodlighting to bid for the slates.

Ian had struck lucky with the timing of his phone-call to Nathan. He had been forced to give up on Gulliver as a tax loss – it was now making him money hand over fist – and he was looking for another way to reduce his tax liability. What could be better than the purchase of a fifty-percent stake in the bricks and mortar of a theatre? So he had agreed to match the money raised by the sale of the theatre's assets pound for pound. By Sunday night the reversal of the theatre's fortunes was complete. After a few weeks of refurbishment and a re-gilding of the plaster cherubs it would re-open in a blaze of glory.

As for Ian, he was formally asked to work for the re-constituted theatre board (it had been re-constituted with exactly the same membership as before) as a marketing strategies consultant. But he declined the offer politely, saying that he felt it would be wrong to sully the purity of his art with things so mundane as money and the market. He was still very much in love with acting, he explained, and expected to remain so for some time. At least until the middle of May…

Fantastically Dressed

Arriving in London at four a.m. in April is exactly like doing the same thing in January. It is dark. Everything is closed. There are no taxis.

Ian – who had spent the previous week at either Stourbridge or Trowbridge; he couldn't quite remember – walked from Paddington to Collingtree Mansions. With his luggage. It didn't take much more than an hour. The building was in darkness when he arrived but as soon as he entered it he was struck by the smell of gas. It was strongest just outside Miss Toil's ground-floor front door. Ian knocked. There was no reply. He knocked louder and kicked at the door. Nothing happened.

Ian ran upstairs, let himself into the flat and opened Mike Pike's bedroom door. There was a sound of snoring, which guided Ian through the darkness to the bed. 'Hey, get up,' he said. 'Help me. I need you.' He shook Mike's sleeping form.

Mike wrapped his arms around Ian sleepily. 'Angel,' he murmured. 'Here you are at last.'

'Mike, I do need you – but not in that way,' Ian said with some irritation, trying to extricate himself from Mike's drowsy embrace. 'Get your lousy mits off. This is serious. Miss Toil's gassed herself and I can't get her door open on my own.'

'Oh God, Ian,' said Mike, waking with reluctance.

'Why d'you have to spoil everything? I dreamt I...'

'Not now, Mike. Look, Miss Toil's dying, maybe dead. If we can't save her at least we might be able to prevent an explosion.'

'A what? What the hell are you...?'

'Bloody get up. I need your muscles.'

'I've got no clothes on.'

'Wear a towel.'

Mike did. They ran downstairs and together broke down the door. Miss Toil was lying on her living-room floor, visible in the cold street-light that came through un-shut curtains. They tried to lift her. Mike's towel fell off. Miss Toil opened her eyes. 'Oh my dear Jesus,' she whispered. 'I need a candle to see properly. Get the matches someone...'

'Not the matches,' said Ian forcefully. 'The place is full of gas. We're getting you out.'

They dragged Miss Toil into the hall. Suddenly Marta was standing at the top of the stairs. 'They're all coming,' she called down, her voice ringing with authority.

'All?' queried Ian.

'Fire, police and ambulance. I've dialled 999. Here's a torch.' She descended the stairs towards them. 'Can one of you go in and turn the gas off? Gracious me, Mike,

I've never seen so much of you before. Perhaps *you* should go in and check the gas. You might find something to wrap around you while you're in there.'

Mike took the torch from Marta and disappeared into Miss Toil's flat.

'Open the outside door,' instructed Marta. Ian did so and the distant wail of sirens could be heard.

'Tell me how you feel,' Marta said to Miss Toil.

'I've never seen anything like it in my life,' said Miss Toil. 'I was born for this moment.'

'I can't think what she's talking about,' said Marta. 'Do you know, Ian?'

'Yes,' said Ian. 'But never mind just for the moment. Here comes the Fire Brigade.'

'Where's the fire?' asked the officer in the doorway. His back-up bristled with hoses.

'There isn't one at the moment,' said Marta. 'But don't go. It could start at any minute.'

The fire crew were shouldered unceremoniously aside by two men in a different uniform. 'What's the problem?' they asked, grabbing Ian in a very expert Rugby tackle and laying him on a stretcher.

'You've got the wrong man,' said Marta, and the ambulance crew released Ian with apologies. They were just dusting off his trousers when the police arrived and clapped him in hand-cuffs.

'I've just lived the moment I was born for,' said a very frail voice from the concrete floor. The police, the fire brigade and the ambulance men confronted Miss Toil for the first time.

'She's the person you're looking for,' said Marta.

Mike appeared from the darkness of Miss Toil's flat at that moment, resplendent in a nineteen-twenties' ball-gown. 'I couldn't find my towel,' he explained. 'But I've turned the gas off.'

'Arrest this person,' said the senior police officer.

'Hold!' came a voice like thunder from the top of the stairs. Everyone looked up. The voice belonged to Max. Max the unseen. Max the bed-ridden. Max was standing at the top of the stairs, hand up-raised like a prophet. With his shoulder-length white hair, his beard that reached down to his breastbone and his floor-length white djellaba he was an impressive sight. Now he began to make his way downstairs. He hadn't used a staircase in seventeen years and he advanced with majestic slowness. 'Hold thy bloody hand!' he declaimed. 'Why dost thou lash that whore?'

'Language sir,' cautioned one of the policemen.

'It's all right,' said Ian, remembering suddenly that Max was learning all Shakespeare's Tragedies by heart. 'It's King Lear.'

'I don't care who he is,' said the policeman. 'There's ladies present.'

'...Strip thy own back. Thou hotly lusts...' continued Max.

'It's all right, Max,' said Marta, going up to him and taking his hand as he arrived at ground-floor level. 'It was a wonderful entrance...'

Max turned gravely to the ball-gowned Mike Pike. 'You sir, I entertain for one of my hundred. Only I do not like the fashion of thy garments. You will say they are Persian; but let them be changed.'

'...But don't overdo it,' said Marta. 'They've got the message.' She turned to Ian. 'I'm afraid he's left the greens.'

'Where?' asked Ian. He was ravenous after his long night's journey and would have eaten anything. 'What greens?'

'The Green Party. He's started up his own.'

'...Let the great gods find out their enemies now. Tremble, thou wretch that hast within thee undivulged crimes unwhipped of justice...'

'Who the hell is he?' asked one of the firemen in an aside.

'Language,' said an ambulance man. 'There are policemen present.'

'This is Max,' said Marta, turning to the whole assembly and beaming. 'He's my oldest friend. He's been in bed for seventeen years. This is his first time downstairs. We should be congratulating him.'

But Max was again in full spate. 'I will do such things – what they are yet I know not; but they shall be the terrors of the earth.'

'Is he an anarchist now?' Ian asked Marta, while Max continued to declaim King Lear's storm scene speeches at the top of his voice to his astonished audience in uniform.

'Not exactly,' Marta explained to Ian. 'He calls it the Free Party. Everyone and everything is to be free, in all senses of the word. Everything except the post of leader, of course, because that's been filled by him.'

'Has he got many members yet?'

'Just himself. He says that's quite good for a beginning. Especially as he hasn't left his bedroom before now.'

'I'm having the most wonderful, wonderful time of my life,' said Miss Toil from the floor. Everyone turned to look at her again. Even Max's oratory dried up in mid flow. 'It's the best fancy-dress party I was ever at. You policemen are really wonderful. Your uniforms look so authentic, even your faces. And isn't that a real fire-engine I can see in the next room? I'd have come as Eve if I'd known Adam would be here too. And surely that must be God who's just come down the stairs. It's quite,

quite wonderful. The best life I was ever at.' Then she closed her eyes and smiled and a stillness came over her as if someone had quietly shut a window.

One of the ambulance men knelt down and felt her pulse. 'She's gone,' he said. 'Just like that.'

'Howl, howl, howl!' declaimed Max, cutting to Act Five. 'Oh you are men of stones! Why should a dog, a horse, a rat have life and thou no breath at all?'

'Come on now, Max,' said Marta gently. 'It's hardly that big a shock. She was a hundred and three. You were hardly close. You hadn't seen her in forty years.'

'Thou'lt come no more,' said Max, kneeling down beside the still form of Miss Toil. 'Never, never, never, never, never.' Then he sprang to his feet and, with an unearthly cry, rushed up the stairs and out of sight.

'Shall I go after him, sir?' asked the younger policeman.

'Certainly not,' said his superior. 'If this is typical of life in the entrance hall, I'd rather not know what goes on up there.'

'Funny,' said Ian to Mike over their Sunday lunchtime pint in The Alexandra some eight hours later. 'I'd never thought of you as a lady-killer before.'

'That isn't funny,' said Mike.

'I don't know,' said Ian. 'It's at least as funny as Max quoting, 'shuffling off this mortal toil,' instead of 'coil' this morning at breakfast. And that in itself was quite amazing. Seeing Max eating. Using a mug and a plate like any other human being. And talking so much more sensibly than last night.'

'Yes,' said Mike. 'I'm glad he's giving up politics. That'll be another weight off Marta's mind. But all this talk of going out and getting a job… Do you think he'll actually be able to get one?'

'Not easily, I must admit,' said Ian. 'Ex-party leaders are notoriously difficult to place in civvy street. Especially when they look like Methuselah and keep telling you they're every inch a king…'

'May we join you?' said a voice. It was Marta. Max was with her. They looked like two people who had never been inside a pub before.

'We are celebrating,' said Max grandly.

'Our engagement,' said Marta.

'Jesus,' said Mike.

'Wow,' said Ian.

'And not only that,' said Marta. 'Max has decided to apply to drama school. He'll need a second audition piece of course. Something to contrast with King Lear. He has it in mind to choose something comic. Maybe one of you two could make some suggestions…?'

Paris Commune

The month of May approached. The string of new dates that Nathan had contracted the Gulliver company for was coming to an end. People began to talk about what they might do after the tour was over. They began to write letters... began to phone their agents and their contacts...

Then Nathan dropped a bombshell. The tour would be extended a little further. To Paris...

Nathan was no expert at organising international travel. But the redoubtable Bunjy managed to come up with a boat train from Boulogne that stopped at Le Touquet, Le Tréport, Dieppe, Rouen, Louviers, Vernon, Maintes-la-Jolie, Poissy, Roissy, Noissy, Moissy, Toissy and Pont-Cardinet before arriving eventually but economically at the Gare St-Lazare.

'Do I detect a whiff of Lamb room?' asked Toby as they hauled their suitcases up the long platform. 'And are we supposed to start from zero again, just because we're promoted to a non-English-speaking region?'

'Give it time,' said Nick, trying to hail taxis outside the station. 'It'll soon sort itself out. Why don't the bloody things stop for me? I can't believe the gestures required are any different from in England.'

'Shall I try?' Linda the wardrobe mistress offered.

'You?' said Nick. 'What makes you think you'll be any luckier?'

Linda raised one hand, agitated her fingers slightly, and at once three taxis were beside her at the kerb.

'How did you manage that?' Toby asked.

'I have a degree in French,' Linda said. 'They can always tell, you know.'

'That's amazing,' Nick said. 'I can see you're going to come in useful. Are you still fluent?'

'Oh yes. I used to be an au pair in St-Tropez.'

'Why didn't you tell us?'

'Nobody asked. When you work in wardrobe nobody ever does ask you interesting questions. So you only ever discuss buttons. It makes for a quiet life anyway.'

'Sorry,' said Nick.

'You'll find though,' Linda continued, quite at ease with her sudden importance, 'that it helps to be a woman in France. Well, you won't find that. But we will.' She indicated Fran who was getting into one of the taxis just ahead of her. 'And Fran speaks the lingo too.'

Their hotel was in the Rue Lepic, down an alley whose wrought-iron entrance grille proclaimed it a fire exit of the Moulin Rouge. 'It doesn't look much like a hotel,' someone observed.

'It's the right number,' said Nick. He looked round for Fran and Linda. 'Will you come in with me?' he asked.

They were expected. A well-padded lady gave them keys and explained things in rapid detail that nobody understood, not even Linda and Fran, and showed them to their rooms.

The hotel was exactly what Nathan might have been expected to choose, though not for himself of course. The rooms were small, quaint and atmospheric. 'What do C and F stand for?' asked Ian, inspecting the water taps.

Toby turned them on and ran the water over his hands for a few seconds. 'Cold and freezing,' he said authoritatively.

Peter's room overlooked a courtyard where a dustbin, a canary's cage and a crate of vegetables occupied nine tenths of the space and three foraging pigeons the remainder Fran's window peered poetically among mansard roofs of blue slate and north-lit artists' studios. Others, less fortunate, had views only of drainpipes. Toby and Michael, Nick and Philip and Ian had come off best. From the front of the building they looked down on the lower slope of the Rue Lepic. It was thronged with people who were either eating or thinking about doing so. (In the latter case you could sort of tell somehow.) There were costermongers' barrows, and stalls in the centre of the road, all selling food of one or more sorts. Even from their second-floor windows they could make out seven kinds of lettuce, twelve sorts of mushroom, eleven varieties of bean, twenty-six species of fresh herbs, seven types of turkey, eight choices of chicken, assorted sausages, encyclopaedic offal, cornucopias of cheese...

One by one the Gulliver company found themselves drawn out of the hotel and into the street as if by a magnet. Here was conspicuous consumption raised to the level of high art. They were quickly seduced. Peter bought pigs' trotters in breadcrumbs, Michael bought Muscadet, Nick got live langoustines, while Fran bought foie gras and sauternes. Ian bought squirming eels. 'People say that speaking only English is a handicap in international trade,' he said blithely. 'But I didn't have a problem.'

'You were buying,' said Toby. 'Selling is different. You can still be an idiot sometimes.'

The audience at the English-speaking Theatre of Montmartre was large, well-primed and appreciative. But when the show was over the company found themselves anonymous and vulnerable, in the streets of Paris, looking for a meal. Montmartre bulged with restaurants, but most were either much too expensive or much too full.

Soon they were back at the Rue Lepic, disconsolate in a very ordinary drab bar. But Fran and Lindy were soon in conversation with the *patron*. 'It's ridiculous, really,' they said. 'The area is full of restaurants we can't afford, while we've got all this food – some of it still alive – in our hotel rooms just across the road.'

'But nothing could be simpler,' said the *patron*, noticing Fran's blue eyes and frank smile and noticing Linda's curvaceous torso even more. 'With the ingredients you have, and with what is in the kitchen here, I prepare you a meal you will not forget. For very little cost.'

The meal took a little time to prepare. The ingredients had to be fetched across the road from their hotel rooms after all. But eventually the company was seated at a long table, made up of all the tables in the bar pushed together, and enjoying a dinner that began with foie gras and hot bread rolls along with sauternes, then steaming choucroute with pigs' trotters, fresh asparagus with butter and Nick's langoustines, followed by Ian's eels stewed in red wine, eleven varieties of cheese, then chocolate mousse and coffee. The *patron* apologised for the poverty of the experience. If only he'd had a bit more notice…

It cost almost nothing, that meal. On the other hand the drinks bill was staggering. But as everyone else was too, and it was three o'clock in the morning by the time they all tumbled out of the place, nobody noticed or cared.

Over the next few days that little bar became the hub of the company's social life. Thanks to the ability of Fran and Linda to speak French they quickly made friends with those regular clients of the establishment that the French affectionately call *piliers du bar*, pillars of the bar. One of whom…

'Ladies, I present myself. Marc de Bourgogne. At your service.'

'Enchanted,' said the young women, bowing their heads a decorous centimetre.

'My ladies, I am antiquarian.' He bowed deeply.

Marc de Bourgogne was a silver-haired gentleman who wore half-moon spectacles on the end of a nose that might have been aristocratic a few generations back. He wore a scarlet scarf because, although it was May, he was still a Parisian. He had a diamond pin in his silk tie and kept his cigars in a tooled-silver case because, although his tastes were expensive, he was still rich. He spoke some English and the conversation that followed his introduction took place in a mixture of the two languages. It appears here, though, in English.

'I know very well your country beautiful but wet,' said Marc. 'I have been there in nineteen seventy-four and still in nineteen eighty-nine.'

'It pleased you?'

'It pleased me very much but there are many things which I still find stupefying.'

'For example?'

'You shake hands only with people you do not know. Never with people you do know. I am ready to admit, all the same, that I do not perhaps know all the facts. I am ready to believe, for example, that English married couples shake hands, possibly, in the privacy of their own bedrooms.

'Another stupefying thing: you have two words – to make and to do – where we have only one. What hours we were obliged to spend at school to discover the difference. But now, actually, I think I know the difference. To do, it seems to me, belongs with all the things in which the English are excelling. To sing, to talk, to act, to fight, to debate in parliament.'

'And to make?' queried Fran.

'To make,' said Marc de Bourgogne, 'is where you English are not excelling. To make a good mayonnaise, for example. To make a good wine. To make a good automobile or a trusty – er – trustable – train. These things you can not. You do not know how to make money and – I speak now to the men only – you do not know how to make, correctly, the love. And an omelette? You English can not make an omelette without breaking heads.'

Mark spoke with too much charm for anyone to be offended, but his criticisms did not go unanswered. 'About the car I can not accept,' said Toby, quickly falling into Marc de Bourgogne's speech patterns. 'You French are not so hot either.'

'Why that?'

'Because if you were you would have developed special models for your domestic market that had no side-windows, rear-windows, rear-view mirrors, lights or indicator-flashers. No French driver ever uses any of those things, so why not omit them and keep the price down?'

Marc laughed. 'But think then how much sport the drivers would miss. To drive in Paris, it is a great sport. To avoid by two centimetres a bus, by one centimetre a cyclo-motorist, to drive away in seeing their faces astonished, their fists raising in the sky and shouting... Ah, what sport! And you would banish this? Without our retro-visors what sport would there be in the Parisian near-miss?' He took a pull on his cigar and a long draught of Pernod. 'They say to us: to drink, to smoke, to eat are bad for us. Leave us one pleasure then: to drive in Paris.'

'You speak of pleasure,' said Fran. 'But how comes it that so many French men – and I mean only the men, and especially the older ones – never smile when they speak to you?'

Marc laughed again, impressed by her blue eyes and fluent French. And at the same moment Ian noticed those qualities of Fran's for the first time. He thought he must have been blind not to have noticed them before. For the moment he just gazed at her, though, while Marc de Bourgogne replied to her question. 'Garlic,' he said.

'Garlic?' queried Fran.

'Garlic,' repeated Marc de Bourgogne.

'Why?' everyone asked. 'How come?'

'I wondered if it was a generation thing,' said Fran. 'Or a class thing. Or something to do with the Jesuits. But I've noticed it particularly in older men. Most of the younger men here smile most amiably.'

'When you are present, Madame,' said Marc, bowing infinitesimally, 'they could hardly do otherwise. But to return to our sheeps... A few generations ago all people chewed garlic raw. Can you imagine the metro, the shops, a business meeting ... with every people smiling? No, no, no. It was not thinkable. Or you chewed garlic, or you smiled. The both – no. But now... What now? We do not (most of us) chew garlic raw in the metro. We limit its use to the kitchen where it adds piquancy to our frogs and snails. But a few of us, just a few, who have renounced the gastronomical habitudes of their grandfathers have not yet learned the charming trick practised by their sons and daughters and by our Anglo-Saxon friends: that is to say, to smile.'

'So obvious, really, when you come to think about it,' said Fran.

'And now,' said Marc, 'I propose you all a glass.' And he took out his wallet to show that he was being serious.

'I wonder why it is,' Fran said some time later, 'that when British people think of Europe – I mean the European Community – they automatically think of France. Even Brussels and Geneva we imagine somehow to be French. Full of baguettes and berets and litres of vin rouge.'

'Is this true?' asked Marc de Bourgogne with an expression of wonder on his face. 'That when you think of the European Community you see in your imaginations only France?'

'Yes. Well, more or less.'

'Incredible! Because it is the same with us. When we French think of Europe we too think only of France. At least here is one idea that our two great nations hold in common. Two great intelligent thoughts the same.' He raised his glass. 'To Great Britain,' he proposed. 'And to the greater Europe that is also France.'

Metroland

It was a triumphant week. The French press was eloquent in its praise and the actors' pictures appeared in all the papers. Ian gave interviews to a number of magazines and everyone ate and drank more than was good for them. But when, at pay-call that Friday lunchtime, they trooped along to the cubby-hole that Nick insisted on calling his bureau their company manager was in a sombre mood. 'There's good news and bad,' he said.

'We'd prefer the bad first,' said Toby.

'You wouldn't,' said Nick. 'Here's the good news instead. The pay increase Nathan promised has come through and so have the extra subsistence payments for being in Paris.'

'Good,' everyone said. 'And what about the bad news?'

'Well, it's only come through on paper. There's been a hold-up with the bank transfer. Apparently it can't be processed before Monday or Tuesday.'

'You mean there's no cash?' asked Ian, wanting to hear the blow fall quickly.

'You've said it.'

'But what do we do? Living in Paris costs a fortune.' Several people said this. Or versions of it.

'We'll sort something out,' said Nick. 'I've only just discovered the situation myself so I've had no time to do anything. But I'm going to see the theatre manager right away. I'm sure he'll be able to organise some sort of advance from the door money or something. Wait and I'll be back.'

In a few minutes Nick returned smiling. The manager would arrange for them to have a small sum in cash that evening and a larger one at the end of Saturday night that would tide them over for the next few days.

They did indeed receive a small sum that evening during the performance and looked forward to receiving the larger advance on Saturday night. But when the interval arrived on Saturday night the theatre manager did not. By the end of the performance he had still not been seen and the company grew nervous. Everyone removed their makeup as slowly as possible and spent three times longer than normal in folding up their costumes. Linda from wardrobe was pleased about this but still the manager had not come. At last they could do nothing but wait, inactive, penniless and silent. Finally the manager appeared. He looked anxious. Immaculately dressed as always, his black hair and bow-tie contrasted not only with the whiteness of his dress shirt but also with the pallor of his usually healthy-coloured face.

'Messieurs-dames, I don't know how to begin,' he began. 'I am desolate. During a no more than ten-minute absence from my office – to attend to a call of nature you understand – my assistant, a man most assiduous in his application to duty and attentive to the last detail, noticed that the cash element of the evening's receipts was still in the office safe. Thinking it a large enough amount to be of interest to thieves over the weekend he placed it in a night-safe bag, hastened out of the building with it and round the corner to our branch of the Banque National de Paris and posted it down the chute. You can imagine my feelings when he told me about this. All the box-office cash? I asked him. Yes, he said. And the coffee-machine money? He nodded his head. And the takings from the bar? Those too. The receipts from programme sales? Yes. What about – I asked – what about the coins from the vending machines in the water-closets? Even, he said, by now nearly reduced to tears, the coins from the slots in the toilet doors themselves. Oh, Mesdames, messieurs, I have done all that I could to help you out of a problem not of my own making. I can do only one thing more. I invite you as guests of our theatre to dine with me at the restaurant next door in a few minutes' time. I have already booked tables in anticipation of your acceptance. And after that I can do no more. For tomorrow, as you know, is Sunday.'

The meal was superb, the portions lavish, the wine abundant, the service exemplary, the ambience perfect and the conversation sparkling. The salade de gesiers went down like a poem, the confit de canard was rich and sustaining, the cheese as headily pungent as a wood in autumn and the soufflé au Grand Marnier more fragrant than a lady's boudoir. But nothing could alter the fact that no-one, ever, can eat so much on a Saturday, even in Paris, that he will not be hungry before Monday evening.

'What about the metro?' said the theatre manager over the final Cognac.

'Do you mean drive it?' asked Michael. 'Or beg in it.'

'Neither,' said the manager. 'I only wish to suggest that tomorrow you might like to sing for your supper.'

There was a moment's silence.

'Busk?' asked Ian uncertainly. 'Us?'

'Why not?' said the manager certainly.

During their first week in Paris they had got to know, and grown fond of, the metro trains as they ran, blue and cream, just below the boulevards. The tunnels were wide and well lit. From the front carriage you could peer over the driver's shoulder at the route ahead. You remarked the sharpness of the bends, keeling over as you tried to hold onto the posts inside, while the steel wheels screamed in protest at their treatment against the curving rails. Coming into the Place de Clichy station, for instance, you could hardly hear yourself shriek.

On other lines the wheels were made of rubber so the trains whooshed more quietly into the stations with an attendant smell of crème caramel. You opened the door yourself with a stiff little handle ('Pardon, je descends,') but they closed themselves before the train moved off after a low-pitched blast of the horn. You could be deep in the black heart of Paris one moment, the next, catapulted into daylight and running on viaducts through the city, crossing the Seine, glimpsing the Sacré Coeur, nudging the base of the Eiffel Tower.

The metro was cheap. To ride on it, that is. But it was inhabited by a world of people beyond the regular one. The unemployed lived in the metro. The embittered stole there. The disaffected defecated. The maladjusted held out their hands. Artists offered their ragged wares. Fences passed off their latest hot deliveries... Into this world the Gulliver company descended, of necessity rather than choice, the following morning.

It was a beautiful May Sunday. A day for strolling in the park, for flying down the autoroute to the coast. A day for the Champagne country, the Midi or the Loire. But today the Gulliver company had to descend the cold escalator and put its mouth where it hoped its money would come from. Fran had a guitar with her; the others had only their nerves to accompany them. It felt to them like the first day of a school term as they mustered on the platform at Place Blanche.

A train arrived. In the first coach a Portuguese band was playing, in the second an aggressive beggar was doing his rounds, in the third a gipsy lady hobbled on crutches with her hand outstretched. In the fourth an American youth was singing a Bob Dylan song accompanied, in a different key, by a three-chord guitarist; in the fifth a woman sat playing a synthetic organ. They let the train go out.

'This is going to be more difficult than we thought,' said Peter.

'We've got to think big,' said Michael. 'Listen.'

They had a huddled conference on the platform and then stationed themselves at precise intervals along its hundred-metre length. When the next train drew in they boarded it strategically and waited, unobtrusive and patient. In the first carriage was Peter, who found himself watching a Paraguayan dance troupe. In the second, Toby and Michael installed themselves while a puppet show took place. (It concerned two American pioneers and a racoon in a bedroom comedy.) In the third coach a drag artist was doing artful things with a boa-constrictor while Fran and Linda awaited their moment. In the fourth a drunk was begging forcefully (he breathed in your face until you put your hand in your pocket) and here was Ian. In the last coach a striptease act was under way to the accompaniment of a barrel organ. And here was the rest of the company.

One minute later the train stopped at Place de Clichy. Peter stepped forward and tapped the Paraguayans on the shoulders. 'Police,' he said quietly, and motioned with his thumb towards the second coach. Toby and Michael meanwhile peered over the blanket that served as a house curtain for the puppet show. 'Police,' they whispered, and indicated the front coach. In the third coach Fran spoke to the drag artist and Linda to the boa constrictor, threatening to turn it into a handbag and a pair of shoes. The drunk in the fourth coach didn't understand the word police when Ian said it to him so, with sudden presence of mind, Ian picked the man up and placed him gently outside on the platform, thus demonstrating one of the golden maxims of show business: get a standing ovation before you open your mouth and you're already halfway there. In the last coach the striptease act and the barrel organ were getting off anyway.

Few things cause surprise in the Place de Clichy. It has seen everything and continues to do so nightly. Nevertheless the sight of six Paraguayans in national costume being attacked by glove-puppets, a naked man trying to cover his confusion with the encircling coils of a boa-constrictor, and a drunk trying to play the barrel organ while two unclothed ladies draped his shoulders with sequinned robes did attract a certain amount of attention. Not, as has been pointed out, because such spectacles were rare in the neighbourhood but because at that moment the President of the Republic was paying an official visit to the station together with the Presidents of Germany and Poland, the King of Spain and the official envoy of the Mayor of Nice.

Meanwhile the train rumbled through the blind darkness beneath the Boulevard des Batignoles and the show began. 'Think big,' Michael had advised and, if in different ways, everybody did. In the first coach Peter opened his mouth and out floated Puccini's *Ch'ella mi Creda*. In the second Toby and Michael staged a swordfight – without swords. It was something they had done at innumerable parties. Each thrust and parry was accompanied with a shouted expletive. Not the usual run of, 'Varlet, have at thee,' and, 'Die the death, thou dog,' but the words to be found on the labels of German wine bottles, which actually sounded much better for the purpose if the consonants were crunched aggressively enough: Kreuznacher, Nacktarsch, Spätlese, Rotenfelser Bastei. In the third coach Linda and Fran sang their own French version of *Rule Britannia* to the accompaniment of Fran's guitar. In the fourth Ian embarked on the series of audition speeches from Hamlet that he'd honed for years but never had occasion to use, and in the last carriage the rest of the company launched into the opening number from West Side Story. The choreography on this occasion would be better imagined than described.

Peter's Puccini programme produced rapturous applause, though his top B flat in the confined space caused some people to throw themselves to the floor under the impression that the train was crashing or the tunnel roof falling in. But they also threw coins in quantity into the hat that Peter was thoughtfully holding out.

The mock swordfight also produced a warm financial return and delighted the spectators. In the third coach the occupants were, incredibly, soon picking up the words to not only Rue Britannia but also Land of Hope and Glory, and singing along. An unprecedented occasion on the metro which could only have been made possible (people decided later) by the blueness of Fran's eyes and the brightness of her smile.

Ian, more cautiously avoiding the speeches of Shakespeare's more patriotic heroes, restricted himself to those of the Prince of neutral Denmark. His "To be or not to be" was heard in the course of the day by no fewer than three film directors, who all offered him contracts on the spot. He was very touched, he said to all of them, and very flattered. However, he explained, his current contract showed no sign of coming to an end – ever. But he took their cards anyway. 'Don't call me,' he said to them. 'I'll call you.'

As the train neared its terminus beneath the Bois de Boulogne the connecting doors were thrown open between all the carriages and the whole company joined hands with the passengers to sing *Auld Lang Syne* while Nick handed out leaflets about the Gulliver performances and Philip expertly removed money from the pockets of those who – their hands being otherwise occupied – indicated their permission with nods of the head.

Nothing succeeds like excess. The company repeated their performances eleven times that day as the train ploughed its dark way from Porte Dauphine to Nation and back again. By six o'clock that evening they were feeling rich as they disembarked at Place Blanche, ready to call it a day.

But as they made their coin-chinking way through the echoing, ill-lit pedestrian tunnels they were ambushed in a surprise attack by a motley assortment of beggars, accordion players, gipsies, bootblacks and banana brokers who, being numerous, resentful and well rested, were able to rob them of every centime they had made.

No bones were broken and no blood was actually

shed. The exhausted Gulliver company was able to put up little resistance and their attackers quickly and expertly made off with their glittering prizes. After no more than two minutes the Gulliver company emerged into daylight, broke, battered and bewildered.

By a very happy chance the first person they saw coming towards them in the Rue Lepic was the theatre manager. He was horrified at their appearance and even more so by their story. He took them to a nearby café where he was able to negotiate soup and sandwiches for them on favourable terms of credit. The café's owner received their story with Parisian detachment.

'C'est la vie,' he said, as he made a written record of their debt to him. 'Everyone loves a winner, it is true. But the winners have to take care never to cross the paths of those who think that the win has been at their expense. A demain, mes enfants... See you tomorrow, kids.'

The Moving Pavement

Soup and sandwiches were not really enough when you'd worked a long day and been robbed on the way home but such was the common lot of mankind and you had only to open your daily newspaper – if you could afford one – or your bible – if you hadn't already used it for cigarette papers – to see that things could have been much worse. Also on the positive side was that none of the Gulliver company awoke with a hangover on Monday. Those too cost money.

Nick went to his bureau early that Monday morning, and the others followed after an interval decent enough to allow the banks to open. When they arrived there was money for everyone, which included all due increments, plus a handsome apology from Nathan. This took the form of roses for the girls and two cases of champagne. The champagne was for everyone, but the boys drank most of it ... as usually happens.

Nathan had never apologised to a company of actors before and he had seen no reason, when it was such a rare event, to do so with half measures. Even his legendary parsimony was on a grand scale, and his pettiness had an epic quality. So the roses were plentiful and the champagne of such a quality that even the theatre manager (who had dined with Cocteau and supped with Sartre) could not recall having tasted at ten o'clock on a Monday morning.

There was no matinee (in the English sense – the French use the word in quite a different way as usual). Some members of the company took the opportunity the free day presented to go to the Louvre, where they looked at the queue and came away again with a point of view on the Pyramid. Others strolled in the Latin Quarter while others explored the antique shops of the Marais and the quays of the Seine. Ian and Fran were alone in choosing to climb up to the dome of the Sacré Coeur from where, without moving further, they could see the antique shops of the Marais, the quays of the Seine, the Pyramid of the Louvre and the Quartier Latin all spread beneath them like a map, and beyond the city's edge they could see the countryside, wrapped in a green and white blanket of may and Queen Anne's lace.

'It's the summer,' said Fran. 'It's really come at last.'

'I have the feeling that this time it's really going to last for ever,' said Ian.

'Really?' said Fran, and smiled. Then she frowned a little and said, 'Hmm. Maybe we should go and find some coffee.'

In the evening the dressing-rooms were full of flowers from well-wishers while the theatre corridors were full of bolder well-wishers, who hoped for a more personal contact with the increasingly celebrated Gulliver company. (For the events of the previous day had made the national press, and questions about safety in the metro had been asked in the Assemblée Nationale.) The curtain rose upon a house that was full to the gargoyles and when it came down again at the end of the evening the audience went wild with stamps and cheers. Their appreciation actually extended the running time of the evening by seven minutes, which meant that the usherettes went into overtime… So now everyone was happy.

The comparative anonymity of the little bar in the Rue Lepic was surprisingly welcome afterwards. And now there was more news from Nathan, which Nick had gleaned in the course of a routine phone-call. There were as yet no further dates booked for after Paris, but no-one was to worry. Dates were looking for Gulliver now, not Gulliver for dates. Nathan had a lot of offers to weigh up. It might be Berlin next. or Prague. An approach had even been made by the Vatican.

Other news was less welcome. It concerned the newly re-named Gulliver Theatre at Robertsbridge in darkest Sussex. Nathan was planning to open his first season with a musical called…

'But without consulting us?' Ian interrupted.

''Fraid so,' said Nick.

'But he promised. I mean, it said in the theatre's new charter that we would be party to…'

'It seems that Dracula found a little loop-hole.'

'Of all the bloody…'

'You should know Nathan by now,' said Toby.

'But Dracula!' said Ian in a voice of dismay. 'He was supposed to be on our side.'

'What a lot you still have to learn,' said Toby in his most paternal tone. 'Are you still sure about your theatre-rescuing exploits? With the best will in the world you seem to have delivered the damsel up to the dragon.'

'Hmm,' said Ian. 'I'll reserve judgement. What's the new show called, Nick?'

'It's yet another version of the Lancelot and Guinevere story. Title: Slender Is The Knight.'

'Ugh,' said Ian. 'I don't reserve judgement. I reverse it. The title speaks for itself. It'll be frightful. Who's going to play Guinevere?'

'Our dear Susan.'

'But what about Pyjamas…?'

'Coming Off,' said Nick.

'But it's only just Gone In.'

'I know it's only just Gone In. But now it's Coming Off. You know show business.'

'Well,' said Ian. 'At least Susan's got something to Go Into. Anyway, who's playing Lancelot?'

'No-one I'd heard of,' said Nick. 'Funny name. Mick … er … Mike Something… Mike Pike.'

'The little bugger!' exclaimed Ian. 'Wait till I...'

'Know him?' asked Nick.

'He's one of my flat-mates. He sleeps with Nathan. I'll swear he does!'

This remark caused a sensation. Ian hastily tried to explain that he hadn't meant what he'd just said: that he'd spoken off the record, metaphorically, hyperbolically, rhetorically. But none of his adverbs were any use. He tried adjectives. He admitted that what he had said was untrue, incorrect, wrong. It was still no good. The more he tried to withdraw the calumny the more deeply it registered, like an inexpertly pursued splinter in the thumb.

Ian began to think that only two things could happen that might succeed in taking his companions' minds off the subject: a terrorist attack or the arrival of someone with three crates of champagne. Happily, one of those things did happen about half a second later and – even more happily   it was the second of the two. Ian only just had time to reflect, first, how readily an untruth is accepted – in marked contrast to its opposite, and second that Mike Pike had once actually told him this – before a bubbling glass was pushed into his hand and someone told him to stop daydreaming and join the party.

The gift bearer was Marc de Bourgogne. 'Messieurs-dames,' he said. 'I was stupefied. To read in my morning paper this afternoon...' Marc was a late riser '...that you were aggressed in such a fashion, not five metres...' he gestured downwards '…from where we stand. The reputation of the Parisian hospitality is in question. This evening you drink as my guests.'

Marc listened as they told him of their adventures underground and then he told them a metro story of his own.

'As you know, I am antiquarian. I have an antiquity shop in the Rue Chateaubriand and also a stall in the Marché aux Puces. Now this happened last month. I was on my way home one evening from the Rue Chateaubriand…'

'Only the French could name a street after a steak,' muttered Philip to Nick.

'Idiot,' whispered Nick.

'And I was obliged to change trains at the Invalides. Do you know the metro station there? There is a long … a very long … er … moving walkway between one part of the underground station and the other. On this occasion the moving walkway wasn't working and so we poor travellers had to do the walking ourselves. Among us was a young nun who was carrying a very big and heavy-looking suitcase. We found ourselves walking along side by side. So small was the nun, so big her case, so long the tunnel and so un-moving the walkway that I began to feel sorry for her. After a bit I asked if I could carry her case for her.

'"That's very kind of you, sir," she said with a smile, "but I hope you won't be offended if I answer, no thanks. You have a friendly face but one hears of such things in the metro – attacks, assaults, things worse than that. You can't know who you can trust. I hope you understand." We walked on in silence for a few more seconds.

'Then I said, "I have an idea. I give you my watch, you give me your suitcase and, when we arrive at the turnstile we can exchange our burdens. Yours will have been much lighter than mine."

"'And worth rather more," she said, taking the gold pocket watch I gave to her.

"'Perhaps," I said. "I'm actually a dealer in antiques. I have a stall at the flea market. This watch came into my possession by chance. It was among the effects of a dead man whose goods I had the responsibility of selling. It dates from the time of Napoleon III. And do you see there are three little gold coins from the reign of Louis XV attached to the chain?"

"'Yes. It's rather wonderful. How much do you think it's worth? As an antique dealer."

"'About forty thousand francs, my dear sister."

"'That's amazing," she said.

'We talked of this and that for two or three minutes, the suitcase weighing more heavily on my arm with every passing second. But at last we came to the end of the non-moving moving walkway, and were in sight of the turnstiles.

'"Wait one second," said the young nun. "I've just caught sight of my mother superior over there. I must go and have a word." And to my astonishment she hoisted up her skirt a good twenty centimetres and legged it at full speed towards the turnstiles. I looked around but could see none other nun. Then I just stood still with amazement, mouth falling open. My young nun had vaulted the barrier and disappeared into the labyrinth of corridors on the other side. Useless to try and follow her. I shouted, "Stop that nun!" a couple of times, but nobody seemed to understand.

'I haven't seen the nun, or the watch, from that day to this.

'The suitcase contained a clean nun's habit, carefully ironed, and six solid silver candlesticks, on the bottoms of which I found well-glued labels bearing the words, "Property of the Abbey of St Martin, Fécamp", and a telephone number.

'I got the labels off with the steam of a kettle and, a little while later, the six candlesticks brought me just under twenty thousand francs. As for the nun's habit, OK, that hasn't sold yet. But tomorrow, who knows? After all, like you say, tomorrow is another day.'

They all raised their glasses in appreciation of Marc de Bourgogne's story. As for whether they were supposed to believe it or not, Ian for one could never make up his mind. Beneath them the ground trembled faintly as yet another metro train burrowed by.

Air time

'Virago,' barked Nathan, framed in the doorway of the Lion room and waving a piece of paper.

'Pardon?' said Bunjy, looking up from the new laptop that was her share in the Gulliver windfall and wondering whether or not the remark was intended to mean her.

'Virago,' repeated Nathan as emphatically as Archimedes might have pronounced the word he uttered when he rushed naked from the bathroom.

'Could you explain?' Bunjy asked.

But Nathan didn't. *Never explain, never apologise* was his motto. Last week he had broken his rule and apologised to the Gulliver company with champagne and roses. He had no intention of compounding that lapse by, this week, explaining something to his secretary. Instead he waved the piece of paper again, like Chamberlain after Munich. 'Virago,' he said once again as if announcing a triumph. Then he withdrew into the Lion room and shut the door.

Paris was in full spring this Monday lunchtime, the beginning of Gulliver's third and final week there. Café tables were blooming along the sun-swept boulevards and waiters' aprons fluttered in the breeze. The Place des

Abbesses was dappled with leaf-light from the plane trees and the air was ringing with young men's laughter and fragrant with female smiles. 'I will miss this,' said Toby with feeling.

The many heads of Gulliver nodded their agreement. They were seated around tables on the pavement, drinking beer that was the colour of the sun and as cold as quicksilver. Some were eating salads, some seafood, some were eating both. All were wearing dark glasses: partly because the sun was brilliant, partly because they could easily afford them, but chiefly because they were now quite famous people and were afraid of not being recognised in the street.

Nick and Philip, also wearing shades, came into the square and joined them.

'Well?' the actors asked. 'What's the news? Final curtain? Or where are we going to be this time next week?'

'I've spoken to Nathan,' said Nick. 'It's all fixed. And the money's great.'

'Yes,' said Toby. 'But where are we going to be?'

'Does that matter?' Nick asked in reply, 'when you're going to be getting…' And he whispered a figure sibilantly across the table.

'Jesus!' exclaimed some people.

'Wow,' said others.

While the rest were struck silent and only their eyebrows, their breathing routines and their pulse rates testified to their wonder at the impressive figure.

'But all the same,' Toby tried again when his own eyebrows had subsided by a centimetre, 'do you know where we'll be?'

'Yes,' said Nick. 'You'll be on a plane.'

'Going where?'

'Nowhere. Just on an aeroplane.'

'What do you mean?' asked Toby with a soupçon of suspicion in his voice. 'It's not going to be another of Nathan's medieval banquet gimmicks, is it?'

'No, of course not. This is the big time. It really is.'

'Explain.'

'You've heard of Virago?'

'The hair salon, the publisher, or the grape variety?' asked Michael.

'None of those,' said Nick. 'The airline.'

'Right,' said Fran. 'I'm with you. It was started three years ago. Run entirely by women. All female air-crew and cabin staff. Doing very well. Best safety record and least ambiguous balance-sheet in the industry. Correct me if I'm wrong.'

'Right on all counts,' said Nick.

'I don't follow,' said Ian. 'What's the tie-up between us and a bunch of strato-cruising feminists?'

'Work,' said Nick. 'We're going to work for Virago for three weeks, starting next Monday.'

'Work in what capacity?' everyone wanted to know.

'They're launching their transatlantic service in ten days' time. With a gimmick.'

'And we're the gimmick, right?'

'Correct,' said Nick. 'Live in-flight entertainment for the edification, not to say electrification, of passengers who take advantage of Virago Atlantic's special offers during its inaugural two weeks. And, as I've already indicated, at enormous expense. Ladies and gentlemen, very soon, in a plane near you ... Gulliver travels by air.'

'Oh my God,' said Michael. 'What will the idiot dream up next?'

'What's the battle plan?' asked Peter wearily.

'Well,' said Nick, 'we don't actually fly till Monday week. Then it's Gatwick to New York and back for a fortnight. Seven round trips in all.'

'And next week?' asked Fran.

'Next week is for rehearsals. As you can imagine, the

choreography will need a bit of tweaking…'

Ian stopped paying attention. All he noticed was that Fran seemed always to be on the other side of the room or the group or – in this case – the table from his own. That the more he wished this was not the case the more Fran seemed to ensure that it was. That even at this distance her blue eyes seemed…

'And of course all this will take place in Tonbridge, where Virago have their headquarters. So you can all get back in touch with your old digs again. Fond memories, anyone?'

'There was this amazing drinking lady,' Michael said a bit hesitantly. 'She was called Holly Bush. We could try her again for old times' sake. Toby? Ian?'

They said farewell to Paris on Saturday night. It was a grand send-off. Marc de Bourgogne presented each of them with a bottle with his name on it, while shutters clicked, toasts were drunk and speeches made. Nathan had planned a lengthy retreat from Montmartre that would involve trains to Cherbourg, boats to Weymouth and more trains to Tonbridge via Southampton, Brighton and Hastings. But Virago waved this aside with polite snorts and wafted them instead on a late-night flight to Heathrow that took only forty minutes and enabled them to catch a weekend at home in London before starting work on Monday. They travelled first class, with champagne and photographers all the way. Taxis met them at the London end. 'Goodnight,' said the cabin crew as they left the aircraft. 'Have a good stop-over.'

Arriving at Collingtree Mansions, Ian was a little disappointed to find that Mike Pike was away for the weekend. He found a piece of paper and wrote on it. 'I'm sorry for doubting you when you told me you hadn't slept with Nathan.' He signed it and left it in Mike's room.

Marta and Max were also away. They were still on their honeymoon. They had chosen Tibet. It was understood that they didn't know when they would be able to return: that it might be some considerable time ahead, but that they didn't care anyway, being totally happy in each other's company.

Paul had sprained a wrist while practising the Brahms second piano concerto and was not around for the moment. Neither was Alice. She was away at Walton on the Naze, in rehearsal for a play about secretaries. Ian had the flat to himself. It was not a very splendid isolation. Miss Toil's downstairs flat was empty still. Mrs Timothy's clients were still going up and down stairs trying to look inconspicuous and nonchalant at the same time. While immediately above, Mr and Mrs Hamooda were busy throwing crockery at each other. At least they were still together, Ian thought, as he mopped up the floodwater in Marta's kitchen. Even the Alexandra seemed strangely empty.

During the afternoon Ian tried to teach himself God Save the Queen on the piano. He managed all right with the right hand but the left one seemed to get odder and odder with each chord change. He gave up. The oddest thing of all was that the flat seemed empty mainly because of the absence of someone who had never been there. Not Mike, not Marta, not Max, not Paul nor Alice. It was Fran who, more than the others, wasn't there. He was glad when Monday came.

'Welcome to Virago and do sit down.' The Gulliver company all sat. They were in the front room of a respectable Victorian village in Tonbridge. The flight-path into Gatwick lay exactly overhead: a fact they were reminded of every one minute and forty-eight seconds. The smartly dressed lady who had welcomed them continued. 'My name is Sally Stockton-Tease. I'm Virago's training officer. I'm also the public relations officer and chief accountant. In addition I'm the co-pilot on the Amsterdam flight every Thursday morning. We are a small company who think big.' Sally smiled and her teeth gave the impression of a small but expensive pearl necklace.

'Much has been said, much has been written,' Sally went on, 'about Virago since its start-up three years ago. One thing on which everyone is agreed is this: Virago is different. In the early days we expressed this difference most notably by carrying only female passengers. I think that most of us would now concede, with hindsight, that this policy, although admirable in its purity and zeal, was, at least in its effect on the first year's trading figures, flawed.

'Since then a more pragmatic policy has resulted in two years of spectacular growth and success, culminating in the launch of our transatlantic service next week Let us adjourn now to the conservatory.'

The conservatory was approached through a door at the back of the house. Nothing surprising there. What was unusual, though, was that the glassed-in structure was the size of three football pitches. But what made the company catch its collective breath was the fact that practically the whole space was filled by a massive, gleaming, red and gold liveried Boeing 747 jumbo jet.

'It's big, isn't it,' said Ian with a bit of a gulp.

'Of course it's not a real one,' said Sally. 'It's just a simulator.'

'What do your neighbours think about it?' Toby asked conversationally. 'I mean, in a residential area of Tonbridge.'

'To be honest, we don't know,' said Sally, 'We don't think any of them have noticed.'

It was an exhausted Gulliver company that tumbled out into the streets of Tonbridge that evening. The choreography was proving difficult and there was still a long way to go. In addition there had been fire drills to learn, evacuation procedures to handle, handles to master, and master switches to switch. Sliding down the escape chutes had been quite fun but the simulated dinghy capsize in the diving tank had proved a chilly experience. Linda had nearly drowned. 'It's all in the course of art,' said Peter as he restored her with the kiss of life… It was something they had been practising, very fortunately, for quite some time.

When Ian, Toby and Michael arrived outside Holly's familiar front door the window was shut, the door was locked, and Toby didn't feel like climbing the drainpipe this time. His clothes had got tighter during his stay in Paris, he explained. So they threw stones at the window instead.

'Who is it?' Holly asked, opening up and peering down.

'Us,' said Michael in exasperation. 'Don't you remember? We phoned you from Paris.'

'No,' said Holly flatly. 'I don't.'

Patiently they explained who they were and Holly did eventually remember something about a phone-call. She came down slowly and let them in.

'It's lovely to see you again,' the three of them said.

'What do you mean, see you again? We've never met before.'

'Never met before?' protested Ian. 'What do *you* mean? We were here just four months ago.'

'Can't have been,' said Holly, shaking her head. 'I've never had stars before. But come in anyway. Have a gin.'

They persisted. 'Gulliver. You know. Back in the winter. You kept breaking eggs.'

Holly shook her head. 'Don't remember.'

'Well, we're here again,' said Michael. 'Whether you remember us or not. Stars or not, we haven't changed. Nothing's changed. Unless you have. How's Jason these days?'

Holly looked at him sharply. 'Ah... He's locked up now. Along with all the other kids. I shopped them to the police. Somebody came here a few months back – don't remember who – and he told me to get rid of those boys and make a proper living from the theatre. By taking in more paying guests. Best bit of advice I ever had.' She smiled smugly.

'I think the source of that advice might have been me,' said Ian a bit uncomfortably.

Holly scrutinised him carefully. 'Nah,' she said. 'Never seen you before in my life. But what does that matter? Make yourselves at home, have another gin and enjoy your week. My bed and breakfast charges...'

'Hey!' protested Toby. 'That's three times as much as you charged us in February... Just because we're famous now...'

Holly looked at Toby with narrowed eyes. 'Are you saying you can't afford it?'

'No,' said Toby. 'It's just the principle of the thing...'

Holly cut him off. 'I don't see what you've got to complain of then. I took some good advice from someone once, and ... well, here I am now. I'm not charging you top whack because you happen to have made a success of things. I'm charging you over the odds because I have. Now, about tomorrow. Who wants the broken egg?'

Poets' Day

'What time's the half on Monday? Ian asked Nick at the end of rehearsals that Friday evening. They had finished, reassuringly, with a decompression drill that involved everyone floating around the passenger cabin in a tangle of oxygen masks.

'It isn't called the half,' said Nick self-importantly. 'It's the flight briefing. It's at oh-nine-forty-five. Only you have to report to me thirty-five minutes before that.'

'In other words it's the half as usual,' observed Toby.

Nick ignored him. '…At the information desk, North Terminal. With passports, make-up and overnight bags for stop-over in New York.'

'North Terminal, Heathrow?' someone asked.

'Dear God.' Nick groaned and raised his eyes towards the cloud-base. 'Gatwick. Not Heathrow. How often do I have to tell you? Gatwick. Gatwick. Gatwick.'

'Only joking,' said the someone.

'Well, don't,' snapped Nick.

'I can see it's going to be a fun fortnight,' said Toby under his breath to those nearest him. 'Give a company manager two pay rises and one pair of sunglasses and just look what happens.'

Gulliver's Travels the Rock Musical, re-choreographed for performance up and down the aisles of a massive, gleaming, red and gold liveried Boeing 747 jumbo jet was an experience it would probably have been more pleasurable to imagine than actually to undergo. Noise, music, drinks trolleys, stewardesses and mealtimes all welded together into a seamless montage. And, unlike the in-flight movies it replaced, it could never be ignored, nor could the sound be turned off.

The inaugural flight was brimful with paying passengers of both sexes, together with a few journalists and the by now ubiquitous photographers. It landed smoothly and on time at Kennedy, with dinghies, life-jackets, escape chutes and oxygen masks still stowed and unused – much to the relief of the entertainment crew, as they were now called. 'Darlings, you were wonderful,' said the captain after the engines were shut down. 'Even Georgina thought so.'

'Georgina?' queried Fran.

'The auto-pilot.' The captain gave Fran a withering look. 'Obviously.'

They spent the night in a hotel called the International Lookalike. It could only be reached, or escaped, by taxi; there being no sidewalk anywhere near it. This was considered a selling-point, as it protected the hotel from the ravages of undesirables such as pedestrians.

'It's a hell of a lot smarter than the hotel in Paris,' said Ian.

'But much more impersonal,' said Fran's voice on the other end of the inter-suite telephone link.

Passenger numbers kept up well throughout the fortnight. The Gulliver company enjoyed its brief taste of this strange new lifestyle and each day seemed to pass quicker than the last. As the captain said, quoting the airline's slogan, 'Time flies – with Virago Atlantic.'

The Gulliver company enjoyed their occasional free moments, their meals in tin-foil boxes, contemplating the waves of the Atlantic as they looked for land-fall, and chatting with the cabin crew. A friendly and approachable bunch the cabin crew were…

All save one, and her name was Syringa.

Syringa was tall and slender. Her long hair was raven black. Her eyes were large, dark and expressive… Though expressive of what it was hard to say. If anyone approached her she would murmur a polite monosyllable and withdraw to another place. She seemed to live on the other side of an invisible wall – like a nun. Everyone was mesmerised by her beauty (except for Ian, who had eyes only for Fran these days) and her beauty was enhanced by her remoteness. Even when she stood no more than a flea-jump away she seemed as distant as the North Atlantic pack-ice they sometimes glimpsed from the port-holes.

'Oh, Syringa never talks to anyone,' the other flight attendants said. 'Pay no attention to it. It's just her way. She means no harm to anyone.'

But on the last day but one Syringa spoke. It was on the outward leg of the final round trip. They were approaching the Newfoundland coast and eating chicken wings in aspic. There were cotton-bale clouds outside with bits of green Atlantic showing between them and there was half a Danish pastry to follow the chicken wings. 'Yes,' said Syringa suddenly, in answer to a question that it was clear no-one but herself had asked. Then she turned her sculpture of a face towards Toby, her eyes dark wells of infinite depth, and repeated the word with a startling intensity. 'Yes.' Then she added, 'But is it Art?'

At first the only response was a stunned silence. But at last Toby had the presence of mind to ask if she was referring to the jelled chicken wings or to Gulliver's Travels. Syringa only snorted in reply. (Not like an ox, but delicately, in the manner of a gazelle.) So Toby took a deep breath.

'All right,' he said. 'Just think about it. Consider the logistics of putting on a show like ours in this jumbo-sized sardine can with – for good measure – waitress service threading its way through the fabric of the production as seamlessly as the metal strip through a twenty-pond note. If that isn't art, then I don't know what is.'

'That,' said Syringa softly, 'is art with a little A. A

little, little A.' She took a deep soughing breath that sounded like the wind through ash trees on the fringe of a coppice, presaging a storm. 'But where, tell me, is the Art with its A in upper-case, in majuscule, in majesty: the Art which nourishes the soul; the Art which sustains the grail-seeking pilgrim; the Art which succours the love-lorn; the Art which interprets back to us our actions, pains and puzzlements and gives them meaning; the Art which cannot be measured by counting semi-colons or tears shed in the closing bars of a rhapsody; the Art without which we are shrivelled, withered and reduced to computer-literate super-beasts, feeling, living, being, nothing???'

There was a silence during which the plane's engines sounded very loud.

'It's a good question,' said Toby eventually. 'A very good question.' He looked around at his travelling companions. 'Would anyone care to answer it?' Nobody offered, so he decided to have a go himself.

'I suppose,' he began, 'If Art has to have such a toweringly big A as you seem to insist on, then there probably isn't much sign of it in our humble little grand spectacle. I guess there was when Swift wrote the original book. But I wouldn't presume to judge even that.'

'Oh, I would,' said Syringa breezily, 'and you'll understand why in a minute. But first, let us look at what has happened. We begin with a book which is a work of Art and we end with a banal pageant in a plane which is no Art at all. What happened in between?'

'Well…' Toby began but Syringa cut him off.

'I'll tell you what happened,' she said. She rose slowly and beautifully to her feet, a priestess rising to give benediction. 'Money happened. Money with a large M. Money intervened and interred all Art. Money which is the end and antithesis of all creating. Money which Counts – with a big C – as a terminal illness. Money which Ranks – with a capital R – as a putrid infestation, rotting all with whom it rubs shoulders or greases palms. Money is the Root – with a capital R…'

'Oh, steady on, for God's sake,' said Toby. 'f you're going to wax innocent about money like that would you mind telling us all how, and if, you manage without it? Surely you don't mean to say, for example, that you aren't paid for your work on board as a…'

Syringa interrupted with another snort, this time as delicate as a thoroughbred foal's. 'My work?' She exhaled the word as if it was a dangerous fluorocarbon. 'What has that to do with anything? What has that to do with Art? You see me, working as a simple flight attendant. How little you know. For I am other than that: different from what you see; poles apart from anything you may imagine. I represent the essence of the intangible. I am… I am a Poet. I see that you are shocked, but it is true. I am a Poet.'

'With a large or small P?' asked Michael.

'Both,' said Syringa, plosive with contempt for

question and questioner alike.

'Can you prove it?' asked Toby.

'Easy,' said Syringa. 'I haven't made a penny piece out of it.'

'I suppose that is fairly conclusive evidence,' said Ian, joining in for the first time.

'Would you say,' asked Toby, 'that to be a poet – irrespective of the size of the P – it is necessary actually to write poetry or is it sufficient, in your opinion, simply to incur financial loss or other hardship from poetry unwritten?'

'A question worthy of an answer,' said Syringa, almost looking pleased with Toby for asking it. 'To be a poet needs no slim volume of verses, published or unpublished as the case may be. Nor does it even require a quiver-full of beautiful un-versified reflections. Just a slim gilt soul walking between passion and perdition. That is all that is required. That and no money connected with it, of course.'

'Then anyone could be a poet?' Ian hazarded.

'Anyone could,' said Syringa, 'but few are. Now, I explained a moment ago that I was a poet with both a large and a small P. I not only have a slim gilt soul that walks the requisite tight-rope but I actually write verses while I'm about it. This is a rare combination, you will agree. Would you like to hear one of my poems?'

'Why not?' said Michael.

'I've just completed a volume of sonnets in strict stylistic imitation of John Donne but I'm not going to recite one of those. Instead I've decided to do one that might be more particularly relevant for you. I hope that doesn't sound too mercenary.'

'Don't worry,' said Michael. 'We promise not to pay you for the privilege.'

'It's called Souk.'

'Souk?'

'Souk.' Syringa fixed Michael with a glare and then recited from memory as follows.

'Kah! Zzzzzzzzzzzzzzzzzzz.

Zeeeeeeeeee. (Kebab. Kebab.)

Hoooooooooooosh. (Ca-dunk. Kung-dum.)

Wheeeeeeeeeeeeeeeve. Pasou. Souk... Souk.'

There was another moment when the plane's engines sounded very loud. And when that moment was past Toby took a deep if prosaic breath and said, in an emperor-undressing tone of voice, 'I don't call that a proper poem. It seems to be entirely lacking in either beauty or meaning and I've always believed that a poem should have at least one or the other. In addition it has no rhyme or rhythm – inessentials, I grant you, but they've saved many a mediocre verse from oblivion.

What's more, it doesn't appear to be in any known language.'

'Well, I disagree with Toby,' said Peter. 'To my ears...' Peter always mentioned his ears with a slight emphasis, as if to remind everyone of his pre-eminence in matters musical '...it does have a certain beauty, albeit of an unconventional sort, not always evident to those with bourgeois habits of listening. And it most certainly has a meaning. That is as plain as a pikestaff. It's all about a cooked meat stall in an oriental bazaar. The stall-holder is shouting his wares and turning his sizzling kebabs at the same time. Onomatopoeically it's very effective. Vivid, fresh, colourful and spicy.'

Syringa regarded Peter. 'Tosh,' she said.

'Pardon?' Peter queried.

'Tosh,' she said again. 'I've never heard such rubbish. The poem has nothing whatever to do with oriental bazaars or grotty little bits of meat. What a ridiculous idea! Nonsense from start to finish. Poets, beware most of all the generous critic!'

'I wonder if she's got many friends,' Philip whispered to Nick.

'The meaning,' said Syringa, 'should be as translucent as a trout stream to anyone. And to you lot of all people. I had forgotten, or had simply not realised, just how profoundly corrupted your artistic sensibilities had become. Blunted like garden tools lost in the compost heap. This poem represents simply the letting-in of a theatre's safety curtain at the end of a play. And you didn't guess? Not one of you? Not even Toby?' She shook her head slowly in disappointment. 'You've sunk to the level of...' She spat the word '...professionals. Why, you're nothing but a pack of hacks.' She seemed to grow as she stood before them. 'But one day you'll see revealed the truth of my poetry. And then you'll be sorry. Too late. You'll be Sorry. Sorry! Sorry!!'

The entertainment crew beheld her, open-mouthed and speechless.

'And now,' she came to the final point of her peroration, 'if you will excuse me I have to go and serve coffee.' And with that she swept down the aisle like a rare and beautiful seabird skimming the waves of an uncomprehending ocean and disappeared into the galley.

Down to Earth

Coffee never came. The purser came on the PA to announce that there wouldn't be any. She apologised, hoped people would not be unduly inconvenienced, and asked them to listen attentively to the captain, who was about to address them on an important matter.

'I hope it's not going to be another poem,' muttered Philip.

It wasn't.

'Good afternoon. This is your captain. We're a hundred and forty-five miles out of Kennedy now. That's thirty-five minutes' flying time. We'll be commencing our descent a little early, in about three minutes. Unfortunately there has been a marked change in the economic climate since we took off this morning. The airline industry is now in a state of acute recession. By this time tomorrow Virago will be bankrupt.

'Naturally we should like to get the plane back to Gatwick tomorrow to honour our obligations. Unfortunately our fuel credit at Kennedy is very limited and in order to safeguard our return journey our accountant has instructed me to shut down the engines in three minutes' time.

'This should be no cause for alarm. Seattle have assured me that the Boeing 747 is quite capable of a one-hundred-and-ten-mile un-powered glide, although no-one has ever actually tried it. Provided that Kennedy play ball and give us a straight-in approach we don't anticipate any problems. Thank you for your understanding.'

About one minute later the quartet of jet engines became a trio, then a duet, then a brief solo, before disappearing altogether like the players in the Farewell symphony. It was very quiet in the cabin. Outside, the wind could be heard, rushing ghost-like through the lifeless turbines.

'I hate to sound mercenary,' Philip whispered to Nick, 'but what about our money? Will we be paid or not?'

'Damn the money,' said Nick. 'We'll be lucky to get down from here alive!' He looked out of the window. The clouds seemed nearer now and more threatening.

'Ian,' said Toby, 'you're the expert in rescuing bankrupt organisations. What do you suggest for our present situation? A mid-air jumble sale?'

'I don't think there's a lot of time for that,' said Ian solemnly. 'And it might be a bit counterproductive if people started demolishing the aircraft in mid-descent. Which tends to happen when they buy a stake in something with a doubtful future. I think it might be best if we did what we're supposed to be best at... I mean entertain the passengers.'

'Entertain?' queried Michael. 'After all we've heard from Syringa about Art?'

'You only have to look at them,' said Ian. 'Four hundred white-faced people gripping the seat in front, or a gin and tonic, or the nearest stewardess. Surely we can do something to help?'

'Of course we can,' said Peter. 'I could do *Nessun Dorma* from Turandot.'

'And I could do "Once more unto the breach, dear friends". That would be as good a way to go as any.'

'Since it might be their last wish,' said Ian, 'why not ask the passengers what *they*'d like?'

Nick organised it quickly. There wasn't much time. Each row of passengers had to agree to a choice. The results were counted. The consensus was the following. Gounod's *Ave Maria,* to be sung by Peter, followed by *Auld Lang Syne* for the landing.

'Seeing as that's what they want,' said Ian, 'it might be safe to assume that that's what they need. Especially as they expect to be dead nineteen minutes from now. I wonder what Syringa would advise?' But Syringa was nowhere to be seen.

So Peter sang the Ave Maria. The effect of his ringing top B flat in the phrase *et in hora mortis nostrae* can be imagined. There wasn't a dry eye in the passenger cabin.

It was decided to leave the final rendition of Auld Lang Syne until the last possible moment. This left time for everyone to write a last letter, will, poem or testament, or to finish the crossword puzzle. Ian took a piece of paper and wrote on it a note to Fran. *Am I being forward? This may be my only chance to say this. I love you. Believe me. Ian.* And he handed his note to the nearest stewardess. So did everyone else.

'We're ever so much lower than usual at this point,' called Nick from his window seat. 'Look at the pedestrians in the streets. You can actually see the expressions on their faces.'

Michael looked out from the other side. 'Don't read too much into it,' he called back. 'And actually they're not pedestrians; they're fair weather cumulus. Though I must admit they look a bit bolshie. But don't worry. We'll soon be the other side of them.'

'That's what worries me most,' Nick said.

'Ladies and gentlemen,' announced the PA system, 'this is your last chance to order drinks from the bar. Cash-only payments. We hope you understand.'

The bar did exceptional business for the next six minutes.

'Please fasten seat belts and neutralise all alcoholic drinks,' came the next announcement. 'We are seven minutes from landing.'

'How do you neutralise an alcoholic drink?' asked Fran.

'You swallow it,' said Philip. 'To reduce fire risk. Then you swallow as many others as you can get hold of, to reduce fire risk some more.' He glanced out of the window. 'Oh God, the pedestrians look as big as clouds now!'

'We're too low,' shouted Toby. 'For God's sake, somebody do something!'

There was a rumbling noise beneath them and a moment later the plane seemed to rise a little. Or at least to fall a bit more slowly. Cabin staff moved imperturbably among the passengers distributing pieces of paper. 'What's this for?' people asked.

'Loss of baggage claim forms. We've just been obliged to jettison the contents of the hold. Right over Harlem. We'll never find it all.'

'Oh my God,' said Michael. 'Our overnight bags were down there.'

'So were everyone else's,' said Nick.

'Yes, but everyone else is dressed normally. Including you. But we're in costume, don't you notice? Our day clothes, money and passports have all gone down the chute.'

'Prepare for landing,' announced the captain.

This was the cue for everyone to link hands and sing Auld Lang Syne. The passengers joined in with such verve that nobody noticed the actual moment of touchdown, which was as smooth as ever could be. Airport ground staff eventually had to knock on the door of the plane when it arrived alongside the air-bridge to get them to stop singing and open up.

'I'll never make jokes about women drivers again as long as I live,' said Toby to the captain as they filed off. 'That was magnificent.'

'It's kind of you to say so,' said the captain. 'But Georgina did most of it. I was too busy singing along with the rest of you. I'm still never sure if I get the right words in the middle bit.'

Nick joined in. 'There is another thing…'

'I know there is,' said the captain. 'It's here.' She picked up a stack of envelopes held together with an elastic band. 'I'm afraid this is where we have to part company. I'm very sorry about this because it's been great working together. Only things haven't gone exactly as we'd hoped. Here are your pay cheques. I give you my word as a lady that they'll be honoured. Unfortunately we have to maximise our pay-load on the return journey so there won't be room for entertainers. Even such good ones as yourselves. We can only afford to carry passengers.'

'Couldn't we even travel in the baggage hold and parachute out over Crawley?' Nick pleaded.

'I'm very sorry,' said the captain, 'but I couldn't allow that. We have to put safety first. Especially during an un-powered glide.'

'I see,' said Nick. 'In that case, since we can't cash

our English cheques in an American bank and it's the weekend anyway, could you possibly let me have some coins for the telephone? It'll lighten the load a bit for your trip back to Blighty.'

For once there were no photographers to welcome the Gulliver company. No press corps. No taxis either. And in the terminal building – since this was New York – their bizarre appearance attracted no attention. At least they were all very happy with their cheques. They spent a lot of time just looking at them. The figures – and the words agreed – were so big. Also, there was not much else they could do with them other than look. You couldn't really eat them. And most of their costumes didn't have pockets.

Ian tucked his envelope into his shoe without even opening it. 'I'm really not all that interested in money,' he confided to Toby. 'But I know a number of long words and I'm always having beautiful thoughts and ideas. Do you think that perhaps, by Syringa's definition, I might be a poet?' His blue eyes blinked hopefully through his spectacles.

Toby smiled. 'I think,' he said without irony, 'that you might be the one thing that's better than being a poet.'

'What's that?' Ian asked.

'Young,' said Toby.

Above and Beyond

'The sky is not the limit,' Nathan barked down the phone line. 'Tell them that. They've been more lucky than they know. Tell them to look at their pay cheques.'

'They've been doing nothing else for the last hour,' said Nick, 'and the novelty's wearing a bit thin. They're all fed up and tomorrow's Saturday. They can't even buy a sandwich.'

'Friday fasting has a very respectable tradition behind it,' said Nathan. 'Tell them that.'

'They don't know whether they've got jobs to go to on Monday. You must give us some information on that at least. They've a right to know.'

'Balls,' said Nathan. 'Young people today don't know how lucky they are. They've spent two weeks keeping fit in an aeroplane ... which no-one has ever done before ... they've had five stop-overs in New York, they've been eating a la carte blanche, drinking champagne, and none of them has even so much as fallen out of a porthole. Six months ago they couldn't have imagined any of that in their wildest dreams. Seeing themselves in the papers day after day, week after week. They're famous. They're stars. Why, I've even heard that some of them have taken to wearing dark glasses. Let them look at the Gulliver Theatre, at Robertsbridge in remotest Sussex, where the artistic standards they set are being so well maintained and where their talents will find a home for ever in the unforeseeable future.'

'That's all very well,' said Nick in exasperation, 'but what are they going to do NOW?'

'Don't you talk to ME in capital letters,' said Nathan. 'I'M the one who uses capital letters round here. All the same, you do have a point. I'll see what I can sort out and I'll get back to you. Don't go far away now.'

'Don't worry, Nathan' said Nick. 'We…' There was a click as Nathan hung up.

They slept that night, clutching their cheques, in the passenger lounge, together with other benighted passengers, tramps and other displaced persons who had nothing to lose but their snores. There had been no word from Nathan. Morning light woke no-one but the PA system did. 'Gulliver company representative please proceed to Information. Gulliver company representative please pro…'

It was Toby who got there first.

'Special,' said Nathan's voice over the telephone. 'Hush-hush. Big money. Top security. No details. Information desk six a.m. Be there.' Nathan hung up.

At six o'clock, still in costume, they presented themselves at the desk.

'Gulliver?' asked an enormous man in uniform in an enormous voice.

'Yes,' Nick answered for the company.

'Yes what?' said the man gruffly.

'Yes sir?' hazarded Nick. The man really was very big.

'If you'll walk this way,' he said.

'Just one moment – er – sir,' said Toby, 'but who are you? Shouldn't we perhaps know a bit more about you before we call you sir and walk your way?'

The big man faced Toby squarely, his chin near the top of Toby's head. 'Was it not explained to you that this contract is top secret?' he asked heavily.

'It was mentioned, I believe,' said Toby.

'Then your questions are out of order. Follow me, gentlemen and ladies.'

'It can't be so secret that we can't see the contract,' Toby argued.

'It can be and it is. However, you can see your payslip.' He riffled through a sheaf of papers that were on a clipboard he was carrying. 'Take a look.'

Toby looked, gasped, fell silent.

'And if we don't want the job?' queried Michael gamely. The big man showed him his payslip. Michael looked and said nothing more.

The man looked at him out of eyes of granite. 'If you don't want the job? Very well. You can refuse. You are in a foreign country without money, food, documentation or even street clothes. We could make life very difficult. Let's just say that.' He shrugged even-shoulderedly. 'You have the right to say no. We have the power to make things difficult.'

'But who's we?' asked Fran.

'No more questions,' barked their new acquaintance. 'Follow me.'

Half an hour later they were on board another aeroplane. Called here, for some reason, an airplane. They were tucking into a hearty breakfast. It tasted good and that helped take their minds off the fact that the window-blinds were secured shut.

'Hey,' said Ian, 'what's this at the bottom of my coffee? I could have swallowed it.' He fished it out. It was a silver coin of some small denomination. 'Anyone else got one?'

The others nodded silently. They all had.

'I think I swallowed mine,' said Philip a bit shame-facedly. In fact he'd swallowed it on purpose to avoid making a fuss.

'I wish we were back in Corbridge,' someone muttered. 'Playing to empty houses for a pittance.' Others nodded their agreement.

Perhaps two hours passed. Perhaps more. No-one had

a watch. The plane landed and another uniformed figure, even bigger than the first, appeared in the cabin.

'Ladies and gentlemen,' the figure said. 'We salute you for your courage, your professionalism and your sang-froid. Your country, wherever it is, should be proud of you.'

'Do you mean on account of what we've already done or for what we're going to do?' Michael asked.

'Both, of course,' said the other, 'but mainly the latter. Now, though, I'm afraid you have to be blindfolded.'

'Blindfolded?' objected Fran. 'That's not in any contract I ever heard of.'

'Just for ten minutes. Security reasons only. But if you're at all worried about the contract, here are cheques as advances on your pay. They might make you feel better.' He fished them out of a small leather folder.

Oddly enough, people did begin to feel better. The paper promises of really serious wealth – drawn on the account of an organisation whose initials none of them had ever heard of – were soon nestling warmly inside socks and under bra-straps. Even Ian glanced at his for a moment before tucking it into his shoe alongside the other one. Quietly they submitted to being blindfolded. They were led from the plane and onto what felt and sounded like a bus. They journeyed joltingly for twenty minutes. Then the bus stopped. They got out. The air felt warm and the sun could be sensed through the blindfolds. They walked a few yards away from the bus.

'Letters,' said a new voice. 'Some of you have letters and messages. Here they are.'

'How can we read letters when we're blindfolded?' Toby asked irritably.

'He's got a point,' said someone.

The blindfolds were removed. The Gulliver company stood on a vast, flat concrete expanse. There was no horizon. The sun beat down everywhere except on the place where they now stood. They were in the shadow of the only vertical object to be seen anywhere: a solitary, rearing, sky-threatening, sun-obliterating...'

'Jesus,' said Michael. 'It's a space rocket.'

'Well maybe...' said Toby. 'With the sun behind it you can't be entirely...'

'Whatever it is...' began Nick.

'That's our future,' said Philip. The words dropped as if made of lead.

'May as well open our letters while we've got the chance,' said Nick, trying for a bright tone of voice. He opened his first. It turned out to be a fax from Nathan. *'I have a great job lined up for you after this one. I can't say what it is yet but it will knock your space odyssey into a cocked heat-shield.'*

'Damn you, damn, you, damn you, Nathan,' Nick said. He tore the paper up.

Toby's message was from Syringa.

'Sorry our relationship started badly. I have a fond suspicion that we could have made good music together: albeit perhaps a sequence of never-ending diminished sevenths, a painful bliss of discord on the verge of harmony. However, you do seem to have sold out, don't you? Once your talent is prostituted for money, where will it end?

'I wonder where you are now. Sold, lock, stock and barrel to a space-exploration agency, I shouldn't wonder. Ha-ha. I'm only joking. Life couldn't take such a poetic revenge, not even on you. Nevertheless I miss your gentle smile, Toby, and your Toby eyes, full of all that would be best in this world. I wish you well and send a poet's love.'

Toby folded up the letter and put it quickly but reverently beneath the arch of his left foot before Michael could see it.

Ian had two letters. One was from Fran. It said, *'Thank you but I'm sorry. Believe me.'* The other was from Mike Pike. It ran, *'Thank you. Now for the truth. I love you. Believe me in this. Nothing else counts.'*

'Hell's teeth,' said Ian to Toby. 'Why can't life be a bit more straightforward? Especially at moments like this.'

Toby had no idea what had been in Ian's two letters. But he rather got the general idea by osmosis. After all, he was thirty-eight. But he had no answer for Ian.

Instead he put one hand on the younger man's shoulder and tried to smile at him.

They began to walk towards the rocket. And while they walked, rumour ran.

'It's the rocket they're sending up to photograph Mars,' said someone. 'We're going along to entertain the monkeys. We'll be back in a year or two.'

'No,' said another voice, more sombrely. 'It's the Neptune probe. And we are the monkeys.'

'In that case,' said Philip, 'it's curtains for us. Final curtain.'

'No,' said Ian with sudden conviction. 'It isn't the end. It can't be.'

'Why not?' asked Michael.

'Because my life is only just beginning to get complicated,' said Ian.

They were now in an elevator. They ascended slowly. Then they were inside the machine.

'I think today will be an awfully big adventure,' said Peter.

Toby grinned at Michael. 'Well,' he said, 'we're off again.'

'Goody,' said Michael, and put his arm around Toby's shoulder.

A moment later Toby turned again to Ian. 'How are you enjoying the tour so far?' he asked. 'Is show business coming up to your expectations?'

'Oh yes,' said Ian. 'I wouldn't want to be doing anything else in the world. I love the theatre. It's so down to earth.' The rocket gave a little shudder. 'And theatre people are so reassuringly normal. Everyone else, it seems to me, is so ... well ... odd, and the outside world is so bizarre.'

This time Toby managed to smile at Ian without complications. He felt a little nervous. But Ian's fresh, blue-eyed face wore an air of untroubled, happy calm. Behind them all a great door fell slowly shut – with a sound like a safety curtain coming in at the end of a performance.

THE END

****

About the Author

Anthony McDonald. has written more than twenty novels. He studied modern history at Durham University, then worked briefly as a musical instrument maker and as a farmhand before moving into the theatre, where he has worked in every capacity except director and electrician. He has also spent several years teaching English in Paris and London. He now lives in rural East Sussex.

McDonald's books are available from Amazon, both in paperback and as Kindle ebooks. Though, if you've enjoyed The Gulliver Mob, there is no guarantee that you'll enjoy the others…

www.anthonymcdonald.co.uk